HER OUTBACK
KNIGHT

HER OUTBACK KNIGHT

BY
MELISSA JAMES

MILLS & BOON®
Pure reading pleasure

First published in Great Britain 2007
Large Print edition 2007
Harlequin Mills & Boon Limited,
Eton House, 18-24 Paradise Road,
Richmond, Surrey TW9 1SR

ISBN: 978 0 263 19502 6

Set in Times Roman 16½ on 18¼ pt.
16-1107-54700

Printed and bound in Great Britain
by Antony Rowe Ltd, Chippenham, Wiltshire

To an old friend, whose life taught her that never trusting, never giving in or forgiving would keep her safe from hurt. I hope life has been kind to you. To Helen, my beautiful friend: I still wish you had been the one driving on that country road ten years ago… then you'd be here to share the joys and heartaches of life with me. And finally to Justin: a true hero in his ability to reach out to others, and keep giving even when life hurts you. You're my inspiration for Jim, my darling son.

Special thanks to my own romantic hero. 24 years together, and still happy. I have the words; you have the actions. Thanks to Rachel and Mia, as always.

PROLOGUE

I have Read this - Good.

*University Graduation Hall, Charles Sturt
University, New South Wales*

"I'D LOVE TO GUIDE YOU to becoming the best
veterinary surgeon you can be, Danielle. Your
marks and practical experiences speak for themselves. I know you'd be a terrific asset to the
practice." His hand ran slowly up her arm.

Danni Morrison barely kept the shudder of
distaste inside. A few vets had come to this
graduation looking for talent to add to their sur-
geries, and this man had just offered her a
dream job—a beautiful purple plum tossed
right in her lap. A practice in inner Sydney,
tending to the pampered pooches and kitties,
with the added bonus of the Wildlife Rescue
she'd always wanted to do as a free service
thrown in.

A shame the price for the experience was far too revolting to contemplate.

At least ten retorts rose to her lips—but which one to use? The one where she'd like to decorate him…with a red-hot poker? The one on how, if she needed a father figure, she'd call her dad? That she only played doctors and vets with men with a full head of hair? Hmmm…so many good lines, so little intelligence to waste them on…

"Hey, Danni-girl, I've been looking for you."

An arm was around her waist before the words, spoken in a warm, rough voice sank into her mind. No man with self-preservation instincts would ever call her *Danni-girl*, let alone touch her. At least none that knew her, anyway. She knew her delicate looks fooled a lot of guys into thinking she'd melt under their macho male protective instincts.

Even as she opened her mouth, something happened. Confused, she looked up at the man whose touch hadn't inspired the usual urge to dismember him, but the most unexpected rush of *sweetness*….

It was Jim Haskell.

Shock held her in place. *Jim* had his arm around her? Jim, who had never looked at any woman but her best friend Laila in the past seven years, and never looked at her at all?

Was the world spinning the right way?

As she stared up at him, lost in uncertainty for the first time in years, Jim grinned, brushed his lips over hers as if it were an everyday thing—*oh, God help me if he unleashed that on me every day*—and glanced at the older man. He seemed unfazed by the older man's perfect grooming compared to his own askew cap over unbrushed black curls, the crumpled graduation gown covering tattered jeans and runners that were as ready for retirement as the half-dead Valiant he drove, its ancient engine held together with paper clips and elastic bands. "G'day, sir. I'm Jim Haskell, Danni's boyfriend." He put out his free hand to shake the other man's.

The man had already moved his hand from her arm, and Danni couldn't blame him. With six-four of dark, pulsing masculine youth before him, he looked pale, overdressed, old and—*short*. "Ron Guildhall."

"You won't go wrong offering Danni a position, sir," Jim assured him earnestly. "She topped the year in almost all subjects, and gets near-perfect scores in work experience. She's a fantastic vet. Easily the best of all the candidates here today, sir."

The man almost cringed every time Jim used the word *sir*, relegating him to the older generation with the simple term of respect.

He'd crushed the other man without a single word of abuse spoken.

And to think she'd always thought of Jim as gentle and unable to fight! He had more weapons than she'd ever dreamed—and he made no enemies in the battle.

"I—I'm still scouting," the man offered, sounding weak. *Beaten.*

"Well, as I say, you won't find better than Danni. I don't suppose you have two positions? We'd really like to stay together... though I can work in a surgery nearby, huh, baby?" Jim smiled at her with the warm, intimate look of a longtime lover, wrinkled his nose and kissed her again...a touch deeper, infinitely sweeter. "Where Danni goes, I follow."

Danni opened her mouth, and closed it. Her mind was blank. Where were all her good retorts when she needed them? She couldn't think of any; she just couldn't *think,* lost in the rush of sweetness, of *gladness* filling her. Jim's touch was so *right*, so perfect.

For the first time in her life, a man's touch made her feel *beautiful*…and it was Jim Haskell who inspired this wild, sweet aching? Yeah, sure, he was gorgeous in that open, sunny way—she'd always thought so—but—but—

Laila's married now, a mother, and mad about her husband. Jim's free…

"Slimeball," Jim murmured in her ear with his customary cheerfulness, when the other man backed off to find another, more willing candidate. "He won't bother you again."

"I was handling it, you know," she remarked, but with little of her normal acerbity.

Even so, his smile faded a little. He shrugged. "I knew you'd annihilate him—but I didn't want your rep to suffer. At least if he takes you on now, it's for your skills alone."

She opened her mouth, but somehow only two words came out. "Thank you." Her voice sounded odd. Husky. *Feminine.* Her gaze remained glued to him, and she felt so—breathless. "That was…good of you." What did you say when someone helped you out? It had happened so rarely for her, she had no idea.

After a moment, his smile returned, and it was warm, intimate again. "You're welcome, Danni. Just consider it my good deed for the day."

"The original boy scout." But again, she didn't sound sarcastic; she sounded—*ack*—breathless. *Feminine*. Where had all her clever lines disappeared to? "I owe you one."

Why had she said that? It was a blatant invitation for the usual male sleaze to head her way as he came onto her....

Oh, get real, this is Jim Haskell! He wouldn't know how to be sleazy.

As if on cue, he grinned, those big, chocolate eyes of his filled with the smile no woman could ever think of as insinuating. "Don't get your knickers in a twist. You'll find a way to give back one day. You couldn't stand to be in anyone's debt for long."

She gasped in a short breath, and choked on a laugh, but she didn't know if it was because he hadn't hit on her, or in amazement that he'd read her like a book. And the honesty she rarely showed with men came out of hiding. "You're right. How about—" Oh, *man*, was she really going to say this? Without even knowing she did it, she'd reached for his hand, her fingers twining through his. "How about dinner tonight?"

She held her breath, waiting…her mind spinning. Had she really asked a man out? Asked *Jim* out?

Please don't say no. Look at me and see this is a never-before event for me….

The rush of exhilaration filled her, just thinking he might say *yes*. She didn't question why it was so important to her, knew only that it was. Staring up at him, she saw the change. The tiny frown gathered on his brow; backing off before she released his hand, he unintentionally jerked her toward him. "Sorry, but my family's here—" waving at the sea of people off to the left "—and we're heading out for a family celebration. First alma mater in the family, and all that. I'm sure your family's here, too. Bad timing. Maybe another time, eh? You have a good one, Danni."

With a grin and a wave he walked away, leaving Danni staring after him.

CHAPTER ONE

Thommo's Steak House, Bathurst, two years later

FINALLY, TWO YEARS AFTER the rest of her class, his best friend had graduated—and all her friends and family, including her husband and daughter, were here to celebrate the event.

After years of thinking Laila was the woman for him, Jim had wondered how he'd feel, seeing her as another man's wife, a mother, and pregnant again.

Now he knew.

The last flare of useless wishes and longings had ended three years ago, when he'd met Jake Sutherland, and known he was the man for her—so he'd helped them come together. His smile tonight was one of genuine joy for her happiness.

He wished Laila the best in life, as he did for his sisters—and he knew she had it.

If he wondered when it'd be his turn, when he'd find a woman he truly cared for from the heart, who could love him back…well, that was natural, right? He was from a big, happy family, and he'd always wanted that kind of love and stability for himself.

A shame all he'd got the past few years was the kind of fun-time girls who filled hours, not his life or heart. Why was it that the women who chased him were lightweights, and the women he really wanted, the kind of girls he could take home to meet the family, always saw him as a brother?

"I'm out. I'm getting some real action."

With a tiny start, he remembered he'd brought Shana tonight. He almost rolled his eyes at her terminology—Shana was twenty-two, but had an addiction to Hollywood teen flicks. He'd only brought her because she'd never been to Bathurst, and she'd begged to come.

Nice kid, but a lightweight, as always.

"Sorry, Shana. I guess it's rough when you don't know anyone," he offered, knowing it sounded lame.

Her pretty, over-made-up face was pouting. "Even rougher when your date can't take his eyes off another girl," she muttered, for his ears alone.

Jim frowned. "It's her night. She's my best friend, and graduated two years after the rest of us. It's only right she gets the attention. For Pete's sake, she's a married woman!"

Shana's brows lifted. "Who, the brunette across from you?"

A lightning-fast streak ran through him, a frisson of *something*—he didn't know what. Slowly, almost disbelieving, he turned around.

Danni Morrison was sitting across from him.

He'd been looking at *Danni*? Danni with the smart mouth and the bitter disgust of all men? Why on earth would he be looking at her?

Funny, but now he *was* looking, it felt natural—as if he'd been watching her so long that she'd slid into his comfort zone.

No. He could never call anything about Danni *comfortable*. Especially not the reaction his body was having to her soft, haunting face. More than pretty, not quite lovely, but delicate, dark and wistful, he knew if he ever had to describe her to an artist, he could have recalled each feature. He could have done so any time in the past ten years.

Why, he didn't know; she'd never treated him with anything but disdain and sarcasm. After ten years he knew almost nothing about her—she'd never let any guy close enough to her to know her. What he did know of her made him certain she wasn't the sort of woman he'd want in his life. He'd always hated the kind of mordant sarcasm she used as a protective shell around her.

Yet, he could drink in her face all night and never tire of it.

Had he been staring at her all night without being aware of it? It seemed ridiculous to him, yet he was doing it now, and it didn't feel like the first time.

"Yeah, good luck with that," came the quiet, mocking voice in his ear. "I'd never have thought a human battlefield was your type. I'm off to find a nightclub. I'll get my own way back home."

Shana picked up her bag and walked out. Jim knew he should call her back, or at least offer to drive her somewhere, but his manners had deserted him. He was too stunned by the fact that he couldn't stop staring at the woman across from him.

Danni shifted on her seat and frowned at her plate of baked vegetables as if she sensed his gaze, or his inner disquiet. Or maybe it was the steak house getting to her…if she was still a strict vegetarian as she'd been during their university days.

She was as ethereal as she'd always been. He'd have thought almost two years in Europe, working, touring and visiting her German relatives would have fattened her up a bit, but she still had that waiflike look to her—the touch of faerie. Dark hair like a waving river down her back, fathomless caramel-brown eyes and restless hands; her features so delicate she seemed lost inside her gentle prettiness.

Until she opened her mouth, that is. Then the notion that she was a delicate woman in need of male protection was blasted apart. She could give an armoured tank lessons on keeping up protective shells. She scared the living daylights out of any man who ventured near her without their defensive weapons raised and ready.

Don't patronise me had been her favourite phrase, among a hundred lines designed to keep the barbed-wire fence around her space from being breached.

"Have I got gravy on my nose, Haskell?"

Jim snapped out of his reverie with Danni's

withering tone. "No, just the usual ice around your heart," he said without thinking—and he could have cut out his tongue, when he saw her reaction. Not that she paled, or flinched; nothing so obvious for the iron maiden. Her eyelids flickered, that was all; but in that moment, a flash of vulnerability shone in her eyes.

Hurt.

Then he remembered, knew why he couldn't stop watching her tonight—and why she was so aware of his attention, instead of ignoring him as she always had before.

Two years ago, at their graduation celebration. Even in the midst of his family's joy at his gaining the cap and scroll—the first alumni in his poor country family—he'd missed his best friend like crazy, and wandered around the hall as if he'd somehow be able to find Laila. Knowing it was stupid, he'd been unable to stop, feeling more and more lost and alone. He'd missed having someone to talk to, to laugh with. He could have taken a date—one of several, he'd always been popular—but none of them were *Laila,* and that day had been too important to waste on what he privately termed a "fluffy girl."

Then he'd seen Danni in the middle of a conversation with one of the many veterinary surgeons who'd come looking for new talent. The man, at least twenty years older than Danni, had been sending out signals impossible to ignore...and Danni's wistful, pretty face had grown more derisive by the moment.

He didn't doubt her ability to handle the jerk; but by the look on her face, he'd known whatever she'd been about to say would have destroyed her career chances for years to come.

And the dirty slimebag was touching her.

Why, he still had no idea, but before he knew it, he'd strolled up as if *she'd* been the one he'd been looking for all night, wrapped his arm around her waist and claimed her as his woman with a cheerful grin. He'd kissed her with the casualness of long-term intimacy—a kiss that seemed to reroute his brain circuits for a few seconds—and then he'd pulled himself together, and extolled her talents as a veterinary surgeon. Within seconds, he'd got the man back onto the strictly professional path.

He'd expected no thanks for his intervention—maybe perhaps more of a verbal assault about how "sisters are doing it for themselves" from miniature Sherman tank Danni Morrison—but instead of either, she'd given him an amazed, sweet, wondering look...the look of a woman who had finally seen him as a man.

An *attractive* man, a man whose touch had made her *feel* something.

He'd never dreamed of getting that kind of look from Danni, had never wanted it from her, either. At least, he hadn't realised how amazing it was to be a man wanted by a woman like Danni until that moment. Seeing her battle-weary face soften into radiance so strong it was terrifying...and it was because of him.

Why had he kissed her a second time? He still had no good answer—except that the first kiss had been so good. And to his disbelief, it had been even more amazing. Scary, addictive stuff....

And then, *she'd asked him out*. And taken his hand in hers, looking up at him as if he was something wonderful....

The kind of look Laila had given him the first time he'd rescued *her*. A warning shout had reverberated in his head, *Get out of here! You'll only get hurt again.*

And he'd made a hurried excuse and walked away. What else could he have done?

He came back to the present, and saw the

change. Danni's chin was up, her eyes glittering defence, her mouth opening to give him the broad side of her smart tongue.

He'd be willing to bet she had another few hundred attacking lines by now, and in a few different languages…and he'd deserve it.

"I'm sorry, Danni, that was a rude and unnecessary thing to say," he said with quiet sincerity. She deserved the apology—both for now, and for two years ago. He'd walked off on the strength of the look in her eyes, when it had probably been simple gratitude. Danni wasn't used to anyone doing anything for her…or maybe she wasn't used to being kissed. He'd never seen her with a guy in all the years they'd been in the same group.

Her half-open mouth stopped there. He should have been glad he'd routed the attack for once, but all he could think was how pretty her mouth was like that—how *kissable*. She was so *lovely* when she didn't use her mouth to destroy the opposition. If he could just keep her mouth busy with other things, such as soft and pliant beneath his…

He swore beneath his breath. She'd been through more than enough pain with her parents' crazy Hundred Years' War. He'd be *damned* if he'd add to it, no matter how lovely she was, or how lost. How *tempting*.

Hardening his will, he turned his head, forcing his gaze elsewhere.

And saw Laila's little, knowing grin before it vanished. He narrowed his eyes at her in warning not to go there, but all she did was wink and whisper to Jake. Jake's sudden grin and discreet thumbs-up told Jim his best friend had relayed the news to her husband.

Laila knew him too well. The vision had been planted now, the seed taken flower. He *wanted* Danni, and only distance—and another willing woman or three—would supplant it. And that was only if he was very lucky; it only worked with the women who didn't matter.

And Danni mattered from the time Laila had told him why she had so many barricades around herself. He might not wander into her line of fire, but he'd never hurt her, either.

Fantastic. Another woman he wanted so much it hurt, and he couldn't do a thing about it. If he followed his normal pattern, he'd be hopelessly lusting after Danni for years—just as he had with Laila, and before that with Maddy Carlson throughout high school. What was it about him that made him so attractive to every woman except the ones he truly liked?

Except that this time, Danni wants you, too. You saw it two years ago, you saw it again tonight. You can have her, and get her out of your system—but there's something vulnerable about her. Don't hurt her.

With a savage curse, Jim jerked to his feet and stalked out of the restaurant.

Two amused grins followed him—and one confused frown. Danni didn't know what to make of it. She turned to Laila. "What's going on with Jim? He's normally so easygoing, but tonight he's like a hissing cat on hot bricks." His face—he had always been gorgeous, in his cheerful, uncomplicated way—had been filled with quiet storms, soulful and yet hot, drawing her gaze to him over and over. And the way he'd kept staring at her—what was that about?

Her dearest friend in the world chuckled, breaking into her thoughts. "I'm guessing you'll soon find out, Danni. Don't forget to give me the goss. I'd like to see my two best friends happy." Laila patted her hand and squeezed it.

She forced a frown to quell the direction of Laila's thoughts. "You're out of your tree, Laila.

Haskell and I have known and disliked each other too many years to change now."

Laila had known her too long to be put off by the belligerent tone. "Tell it to yourself, babe. The heated looks between you have been flying thick and fast all night." She sighed and rubbed her belly. "Junior's very active tonight. It's all his father's fault."

"*His* father?" Jake and Danni asked at the same moment, with sly smiles. It was a regular joke after the birth of her very feminine daughter Ally, whom tomboy Laila had been so certain would be a boy.

Laila mock-glared at them each in turn. "Yeah, yeah, rub it in, both of you. Have your fun, while I suffer under the kick zone here."

Danni dragged in a quiet sigh of relief that Laila dropped the Jim-topic. After the moment of unbearable sweetness two years ago and his sudden abandonment, she knew better than to *think* of how Jim had just been looking at her.

Except that she *was* thinking of it.

Beneath the table, she clenched her fists. What *was* it with her? She should know better than to hope—so why did she? He'd rescued her once—so what? It was in Jim's nature to rescue people. And if for a short time she'd felt something for him…*hoped*, as she'd never done before with any man…that moment had shattered when he'd made his excuses and bolted at a gazillion miles an hour, as if she'd threatened him with slow torture.

It was no big deal. If nothing in her life had prepared her for Jim's brand of kindness without agenda, or the unexpected hot sweetness that burst through her at his touch, she could handle it now. Over eighteen months of distance— crossing the world to get that distance—might not have replaced him, but at least she could see the truth right in front of her.

Some people were born for love and happy endings. It was not for her. She'd known that from the age of eight, when she'd tried to play Barbie and Ken with the other girls. Her dolls had always got embroiled in sarcasm matches and screaming rows. Her friends had thought it hilarious, but even at that tender age, some deep-buried part of her had known she wasn't normal. She didn't know how to give or receive love like the other girls. She didn't know how to be happy, or to trust in any rare moments of joy lasting. Not for her.

It wasn't in the genetics. She and Laila couldn't be more opposite, let alone she and Jim—and that was leaving out all the things they did differently, like their work methods and their diets. Laila and Jake's entire clan was here, singing family celebration songs, vying for the privilege of holding little Ally. Jim's family was big, noisy and loving, and they all made the trek down here to celebrate Jim's every achievement, coming over four hundred kilometres from the back of beyond to be with him.

Danni had chosen this university because it was three hundred kilometres from Sydney— and her home. Her parents had come to every one of her milestones, but had sat at opposite ends of the room and competed with icy precision for her attention.

No, not for her *attention,* for her to listen: they needed to spill their latest complaints about each other into her unwilling ears.

She was all they had, she knew that. Yet she'd only seen her parents once since she'd returned from Germany three months before.

The visit had ended after only two hours. Having gained space from them during her time in Europe, enduring their constant harping and sly, nasty comments about each other had been more than she could tolerate. After more than twenty years, she'd finally lost it.

Why don't you separate and find your own lives? she'd said as she'd headed for the door. *You should have done it when I was little, then I wouldn't be so screwed up now. You didn't stay together for my sake, you just want to keep punishing each other forever. I can't stand any more. I'm your daughter, not your referee!*

Since that day, her mum and dad had phoned her every day as usual, but although they'd tried apologising, asking, and finally begging her to come home, she couldn't force herself to go back. If she had to hear one more snide, sarcastic remark between them…it felt as if she were dying of slow suffocation, a strangling of her spirit. It might entertain them, but it only *hurt* her, and reinforced the reasons why she'd never be normal.

She came out of her reverie to the realisation that something was wrong. By instinct, her gaze swerved to the large French doors leading onto the back veranda.

Jim stood leaning against the doorway talking into his phone, looking at her, yet it was as if she wasn't there; his whole concentration was on the call. His body was taut, his face filled with quiet storms.

It was none of her business.

She turned her eyes back to the table, determined to show everyone that she didn't care. She forced a smile to her face, and joined in the laughter and teasing common to their group of friends, but rare for her.

She couldn't do it. Just as she always responded to wounded creatures in distress, she had to look at him…she had to *know*.

He no longer leaned on the doorpost, but stood rigid in the doorway, his face so hard it seemed carved in dark marble. His laughing eyes were like flint; his nostrils were flared. She'd never seen laid-back Jim look so shocked, or so thoroughly furious. And the *pain* inside the depths of those coffee-dark eyes…

He flipped his phone shut, turned on his heel and stalked back outside. She could almost feel little flicks of lightning following in his wake.

"Go to him," Laila whispered.

Shocked, Danni stared at her friend. "Me? Jim and I aren't even friends. *You* should be the one to help him. He *loves* you. He'll accept your help."

Laila's eyes grew misty with tears. "I can't." She lowered her gaze for a moment. "I've been having the Braxton-Hicks contractions all day, on and off. I have to rest…and—and…" she sighed, her face filled with the wretchedness of guilt. "*Please*, just go to him. Make sure he's all right—for me?"

Laila was hiding something from her, but the plea was genuine.

All her life, Danni held aloof from people; to grow too attached only caused pain. But from the time they'd met, Laila wouldn't *be* held at a distance. Her open, loving heart didn't know boundaries. She'd dragged the sarcastic loner Danni into her small circle and, seeing the hurt others caused Laila with the *princess* tag given to her as the only and most cherished daughter of an obscenely wealthy man, Danni had begun leaping to her friend's defence before she'd even known Laila *was* a friend.

Laila was part of her heart now, and she asked so little. How could she refuse?

With a small smile, she walked out to find the man she wanted never to speak to again—at least not without her shield of protective sarcasm.

But that was what she had to do now, for Laila's sake…and maybe for her own. If she did a good deed for Jim Haskell in return for his two years before, whatever it was she felt for him—lust, obligation—would be over.

* * *

The phone rang again almost as soon as he'd shut it, and again and again. He just kept disconnecting. He'd be *damned* if he'd answer it. The woman was demented!

Was he part of some prank? It was ridiculous, like some melodramatic movie or reality show. And he'd laugh if—if—

If her story hadn't been so plausible.

That was the worst part of it. He'd tried to scorn the woman—Annie, she'd said her name was—or laugh at her, or think she'd got the wrong number. But she'd named his parents, his hometown…and she'd asked the fatal question.

"Haven't you ever wondered why you're lighter-skinned than your parents?"

He ground out a savage curse. The woman might be crazy, but she'd known a lot about his personal life, including the wonder most kids had who didn't strongly resemble their parents. *Am I adopted?*

Why now? Why had she called? What did she want from him?

"Jim?" The question sounded halting, uncertain. With a sense of fatality, Jim turned from the tree where he leaned with a balled fist. Only one woman he knew had a voice that made him think of shadows and moonbeams. Only one woman didn't give him the nickname Jimmy, and never had.

She stood ten feet from him, seeming smaller than her five-six or seven because she was so dainty. Her pale skin glistened in the clear moonlight; her long, shimmering waves of hair blew around her in the gentle breeze like the ocean at night. Her filmy silver skirt caught in the gusts, softly billowing. Her eyes, fixed on his face, were limpid pools of concern.

She looked like an elf maiden straight from his favourite fantasy books. So *beautiful,* and she had no idea of it…

"Danni," he said with grave courtesy. Hiding his emotions, his need, as he always had. The oldest of six kids, he'd always been the dependable one in the family.

His fists clenched. *Family…* Were they that anymore? His one anchor in life had crumbled before his eyes, vanishing without warning.

"What can I do for you?" he managed to say with a semblance of politeness.

"Laila's worried about you," she said quietly.

"We saw you take the phone call…and your reaction to it."

That was Danni, never hiding behind pretty words; she always got straight to the point. "I'm fine," he ground out, sounding almost savage. "Go back and tell Laila I'll be in soon."

She should have turned and gone back inside—his rare brusqueness had that effect on people—but she stood her ground. "I wouldn't be able to reassure her, and she'd only get more worried. I can stand a lot of things from people, but I always know when someone's lying to me…and Laila will know, as well. I can't lie to her."

"So I'm not fine," he snarled, surprising even himself with his sudden hostility. "What do you care? You don't even like anyone here but Laila."

"True." Her smile was remote, austere. "And I won't have her worried right now. She's in pain and trying to hide it for the family's sake. I can't go in there and say 'He said he's fine, now leave him alone.' You know she loves you. She's worried about you."

A sudden shaft of bitterness hit him. If Laila had loved him enough, he would have her to share this with. He wouldn't feel so scared or so *alone.*

"Yeah, Laila loves me. Just like my sister. It's wonderful." Though he knew the bitterness would fade as quickly as it came, he still said it, wanting to push Danni away, make her turn and flounce back into the restaurant, safe inside her anger and mistrust of all men.

Again she surprised him by holding her ground. "It's more wonderful than you know. You take all the love in your life for granted. I always wanted a sister, a brother—anyone to be there for me the way your family is for you. The way *Laila* is there for you."

The unconscious reminder inside her words cut him all over again. *Family.*

"Excuse me, would you?" Without waiting to see what she did—he could count on Danni walking away in stiff-necked pride, rather than be unwanted—he called home.

A soft, feminine growly voice answered in moments. "Hello?"

"Mum?" he said, feeling for the first time the utter *comfort* of that word; for the first time, not accepting it as his right. *You take all that love for granted.* "It's me."

"Kilaa," she cried, using his totem Aboriginal name: the galah, a big white bird—the one

who'd flown away. "Are you all right? Seeing Laila again, it hurts, huh?"

Though a dim part of him knew Danni was still listening, the tide of emotion, repressed and held in, spilled over. "I just got a call from a woman named Annie. She claims she's my *real* mother."

A stifled gasp was his only answer for a few moments…moments that stretched out to almost a minute. "Kilaa…" she finally said, her voice weak. Shaking. "Let me explain…"

But she didn't. He could hear the quiet sobs from the other end of the line.

"It's…true?" he asked through stiff lips.

One word came and it shattered his world. "Yes."

"Who is she?" The words came without his knowing they were there.

"She's my sister—my half sister. My mum had her before she met my dad."

He frowned. It felt unbelievable to him—his family was too close. "Then why haven't I met her before? Why hasn't she come to any family parties and stuff?"

"We always invited her, Kilaa. She never came." His mother—*except she's not my mother*—spoke in a slow, teary voice. "She was taken away by the authorities when she was two, because she was half-white. She came back at twenty or twenty-one with you. She said she couldn't afford a baby—but really, she couldn't handle it."

"Why not?" he asked, but given his knowledge of their people's history—he'd done a semester of it in second year—he thought he knew.

"She was raised in an institution. I think being with us only reminded her of what she'd never had in life, poor Annie." His mum sighed. "Anyway, she gave you to me—I was only nineteen then— and then she left. I was already with your father. He said, 'So he'll be our firstborn.' And you were to us. You were always our firstborn." Her voice was thick with tears. "Kilaa, come home, let us explain to you. You are still our son."

Jim heard the words, but barely took them in. *So Dad isn't my father, either. My grandfather isn't my grandfather, my brothers and sisters are—are my cousins….*

Suddenly he wished he was a vegetarian like Danni; the steak he'd eaten for dinner sat like lead in his stomach. His knees were shaking, his head spinning.

The bottom was falling out of his world. Half

an hour ago, his unwanted attraction for Danni was tragic to him.

What a difference a phone call makes, he thought grimly.

CHAPTER TWO

"I DON'T WANT TO HEAR THIS over the phone. Expect me in a couple of days. I'll arrange a locum for the practice." He flipped his phone shut and leaned against the tree with a clenched fist. Scraping his knuckles raw hitting the rough bark, over and over.

As she watched him hurting his bleeding hand far less than the pain in his heart, Danni had absolutely no idea what to do. What *can* you say, when a man has his entire life stripped from him in the space of five minutes?

She was useless here. More than anything she wanted to turn tail, run inside the restaurant and send Laila out here. She was Jim's best friend; she always had something unexpected and wise to say, or at the very least, she'd hold him close and *be* here for him.

Which would only be another reminder of something he's lost.

It looked like she was it, then, God help her. What did she say? How did she start?

A moment later, he stopped hitting the tree. "I know you're still there," Jim said, his back stiff. "I can hear you breathing. I can feel the indecision jumbling around in your head."

That was Jim—the only man she'd ever known who didn't treat her with wary diffidence because he'd never been frightened by her fighting reflex or sarcastic tongue. He treated her like every other woman he knew, with teasing and truth. With the respect he gave to all women.

The only man she'd never been able to feel cynical about…at least until he'd ended her most private hopes before they'd truly begun.

But all that was past. He needed help now, and she was the only one around.

She stepped forward. "I'm sorry, Jim." The words sounded stilted, even to her.

Using only one shoulder, he shrugged. Was he blocking her off, or unable to speak about it? She didn't know. She didn't know him well enough to judge.

What an ironic commentary on my life, consi-

dering I've known the man, been in the same circle of friends with him ten years.

"Your real mother called?" She wanted to hit herself for the stupid question, but she had to start somewhere, and she had no idea of how to reach out to him.

Still leaning against the tree with a balled fist, he nodded.

What did she say from here? More inane questions to force him to talk—or did she give him the peace and space to think?

To grieve, you mean.

Yes, she understood that—from personal experience.

"Um, do you want me to get Laila?" *I'm no good here. I shouldn't be involved in this.*

He didn't answer; but in his stillness and silence, his stiff stance, she still felt the waves of *need* coming from him. He didn't want to be alone; but being Jim, he didn't know how to ask for help.

What could she do?

Forcing her feet to move, she walked to him, doing what Laila would have done. Reaching out to him, lifting her hand to touch his shoulder, hoping it was enough. That *she* was enough, because no one else had bothered to come out to see if he was all right, if he needed anything.

Not one of Jim's many friends had come to him.

She frowned. *Why* hadn't they come out? Jim would have done so for them—he *had* done it, whenever any of them needed him. Laila was the only one with a valid excuse—and she was the only one fretting over his welfare, or had even noticed his pain.

At the touch, he turned his face and looked down at her. His eyes were shattered.

"Oh, Jim," she breathed. Though she was wading waist-deep in a stormy ocean of the things she'd always avoided before—vulnerability, emotional attachment to a man—she worked on an instinct she didn't know she had, tugging him toward her.

Wanting to comfort him.

With a muffled sound, the tortured moan of an animal caught in a trap, he grabbed her and hauled her hard against him, dragging in ragged breaths.

A drowning man holding onto a leaky life preserver. Wishing she knew how to help, she sighed and gave up, wrapped her arms around him and let him *be.*

Six foot four of raw masculinity surrounding her had a swallowed-alive feel to it. The hot, sweet tenderness so foreign to her two years before when he'd held her returned in a rush. The jumble of changes in her life in a single hour left her humbled, confused and *wanting* all at once. She didn't know what to do with the inner whisper telling her she was in the right place at the right time.

Yet somehow, her silence wasn't wrong or pitiful. Maybe quiet was what he needed far more than her imperfect words. After all, words had just torn his life apart.

They stood locked together for a long time. The quiet shimmered with peace, like sunlight on a winter pond, gentle and beautiful. Though she'd never done this with a man before, standing in Jim's arms, holding him close and giving him comfort felt so natural she almost forgot to question it, to remember the differences between them.

Perhaps that was the reason: the biggest differences between them had been removed. The rug of secure family had been pulled out from beneath his feet, while she'd never *had* a rug. Suddenly opposites had become two of a kind—

but the welter of confusion, fury and unexpected grief had blinded him. He'd need a guide to walk him through the darkness.

And she knew that darkness well: the parental lies and omission; feeling as if you don't belong anywhere; feeling lost and alone. She'd walked in that darkness ever since the day she'd realised other kids' mummies and daddies actually *liked* each other. They didn't all buy separate groceries, use the kitchen at different times and sleep in separate bedrooms. They didn't all *stay together for the sake of the child*, living in a trap of semi-polite hatred and needle-fine insults.

Some parents *loved* each other.

Some parents didn't lie to their kids—and gentle, honest Jim had just discovered, at age thirty, that he'd lived a lie all his life. He'd *been* a lie all his life.

Slowly, the stiffness in him softened. He still clung to her, but it felt more relaxed, sharing rather than the drowning man's hold. She could breathe again.

"Thank you," he murmured against her hair.

"You're welcome," she murmured back, feeling her hair move, and his breath touch her skin. She shivered.

He lifted his face and looked at her, those dark eyes filled with turbulence; and yes, the wanting she couldn't help feeling for him, even here and now, it was there in his eyes, too. Even though she knew Jim was an expert in playing the game—he'd had girls hanging off him for as long as she'd known him—in the reflection of the deep blackness of his eyes, she still felt beautiful, truly *desired* as a woman for the first time.

And she felt—vulnerable. Feminine. Lost, but happy to be so…and her lips parted…

"I don't know who I am anymore."

Danni blinked, trying to reorient herself. The kiss they hadn't shared had seemed so *real,* she felt as if he'd wrenched it from her—just as she'd felt it two years before when he'd turned her down and walked away without looking back.

Tonight had been a terrible shock for him, she admonished herself. He needed time to adjust, not kisses, biting wit or sharp-tongued defences: he needed a *friend.* She couldn't leave him alone with this.

As alone as I've been all my life…and I survived it, didn't I?

Yeah, you're a regular poster girl for personal growth.

After long moments, she said tentatively, "You should go home, talk to your—" She stopped there, uncertain what to call them now, the people who'd raised him and loved him.

His smile was a grim travesty of the open, cheerful, *I know who I am and where I belong* smile that had ticked her off all these years…and yet now, it hurt that he wasn't the same man he'd been an hour ago. "It's okay to call them my family. Apparently I'm still related."

Wondering how he fit in now, she smiled back at him. "That's good."

"Half nephew," he said, reading her thoughts without difficulty. "If there's such a thing as a half nephew."

"Well, that's good…isn't it? I mean, you still belong with them." She closed her mouth, cursing her stupid tongue—and her body. His touch, the depth of his gaze on her was stirring her senses so much she couldn't think. She'd been thrown without warning into a world where she wanted so much more than to best a man at the game he played, a world without superficial rules.

Maybe it was because Jim was incapable of playing games tonight; he was in too much pain to handle it. She had to ignore her pathetic wish that she could have been in his arms an hour before the phone call had rocked his life off its secure foundations.

"I suppose I do still belong." He kept *looking* at her. His hands, at her back, moved a little. The most tentative caress she'd ever known.

She felt her breath catch again. Looking at him became dangerous, yet she couldn't stop. What was he doing? What did he want from her: a friend to understand his pain, or a lover to help him forget for a while? The thought sent a shudder of longing through her.

Did she follow his lead, or ignore it? She didn't know; all she knew was she couldn't breathe again, and her gaze clung to his.

"I have to go," he whispered, but held her still.

Without breath or balance, she nodded again, not trusting her voice. Wanting too much. *Craving.* She rested her hands against his chest, trying to find the strength to move.

"I want you, too, Danni," he said quietly, giving her the words she didn't know she was aching to hear until they came. "Right now I don't think I've ever wanted a woman more. But until I know who I am, I can't give you what you need."

From another man, the words would have brought out her fighting spirit. *She* didn't need anything from a man. She would make her way alone, and succeed.

From Jim, it was raw truth, he was hurting too much to tell her anything else.

She didn't want to think about whether he was right or not. "So you can't give your usual one hundred and fifty percent. Maybe it's time someone gave to you, Haskell," she said, hearing the huskiness of desire in her voice. "I don't think you should go home alone."

He tipped up her chin, his gaze searching her face, so taken aback by her words, his brows met in a frown. "Are you offering to come with me?"

Amazed that she actually was, she nodded... and made a soft, purring sound when his hand caressed her back, and the other moved beneath the sensitive skin at her chin.

He made a helpless gesture, a little shrug that conveyed his confusion. "Why?"

How to answer that, when she didn't know herself? "I owe you for saving my butt two years ago. And I've been where you are, in a way," she said, hearing the soft breathlessness thrumming through each word. "I might not be adopted, but I've spent my life wishing I was." She looked up at him, half-defiant. "You know my story. I suppose everyone does. I've been navigating the waters of parental lies and self-delusion all my life. You can't let them to fluff you off with their version of the story—and believe me, they'll try. Even the best parents hate being caught out lying or being in the wrong. They should have told you years ago, and given you the chance to find your real parents." She drew a deep breath after saying more in one go than she had for years. "You shouldn't be left alone with this."

"What about your job?"

She shrugged. "I quit three weeks ago. I've only been doing locum work until I find the right practice. So I'm free to come with you."

"How about where you live? Laila said you signed a lease on a place in Sydney?"

She shrugged. "My stuff's there. A week's rent's no big deal." She frowned as he began to find another objection. "Look, I'll come if you want me to. I may not be Laila," she added tartly, "but I'm free for another week or two. I don't see anyone else offering to be your support person."

Why on earth am I pushing this?

As if he'd heard her thought, a brow lifted. "And…? Come on, Danni, say it."

She bit her lip over a crazy urge to smile. She ought to have known he wasn't going to let her leave it unsaid, or let her hide behind her sarcasm. Typical of Jim—but she knew whatever she gave to him now he'd give back tenfold, because he always did.

The thought of what he'd give her, what she'd been wanting from him from the first moment he'd touched her at graduation two years ago, made the sweet wanting bloom into a hot ache in every part of her body.

Wrong time, wrong place, probably the wrong people as well… But she didn't care.

"And because…" She lifted her chin and said it outright, "I don't want you to walk away again and leave whatever this is between us hanging for another two years."

He laughed then—not with his whole heart, not as cheerful as the past—but still he'd laughed, and she'd done it for him. She felt a little glow of pride. This reaching out and doing things for people actually felt pretty good—at least, it felt good with Jim.

When he spoke, the warm laughter was still

there…but so was the desire. "Spoken like the straight-from-the-hip woman you are."

"Is that bad?" She moved her hands on his chest.

His eyes darkened. "It's good, Danni. It's damn good. I didn't think you'd ever admit to it." He pulled her closer. "Come on, little fighter. Make it real."

Maybe he wanted her; maybe he just wanted *one* piece of good news tonight, or a distraction from the knock he'd suffered. Maybe he was lying to himself—but he was too honest to do that. And he'd been looking at her *like that* before the call.

She didn't question why, after a lifetime of denial with men, she *wanted* to say this, and now; she only knew she must, or he wouldn't kiss her. Her hands caressed up his chest to his shoulders; then, the ache of her yearning made truth imperative. She pulled at him, trying to bring him down to her. "I want you, Haskell, all right? I want to be with you."

That gorgeous, big-as-the-Outback grin she'd always hungered to see even as she'd pretended to hate it, spread across his face. "Now say the rest of it," he whispered, resisting her pull, forcing her out of all hiding. Making the thing between them as honest as it was inevitable.

"*All right.* I've wanted you for two years." She sighed impatiently, tugging harder. "And waiting for you to touch me again is making me crazy. So shut up and kiss me. Then maybe we can get back to being friends."

He leaned down into her and nuzzled her hair. "We've never been friends, Danni. You never let me in," he murmured in a warm, blurry voice, thick with desire.

Why did he think she hadn't? She'd wanted this for so many years, ached for it, and getting close to him wasn't an option when he was never close enough.

Need was pain now. She couldn't think beyond him, his touch, his closeness that wasn't close enough. "Now, Haskell, or I might have to kill you."

With a low chuckle he turned his face, trailing his lips over her ear, her cheek and jaw…and she purred in the purest pleasure she'd ever known.

Hearing Danni making the little, feminine sounds of desire—*how the hell has she wanted me for so long?*—drove Jim almost out of his head; yet still he took his time, keeping his kisses slow, gentle and arousing. He tasted the silky skin of her jaw down to her throat. So soft and sweet…she tasted like rich, creamy ice cream.

He'd always had an unquenchable greed when it came to ice cream.

Did her mouth taste the same? He had to know—and she was turning her face, seeking his mouth in blind want. With a groan, he lifted her up against him—so small and sweet, this Danni; how could he ever have compared her to a Sherman tank?—and let it happen.

Bam.

He'd known for years he had the hots for Danni—what guy wouldn't, given her delicate loveliness, the challenge of her defences and battleground intellect?—but he'd dismissed it as an inconvenient desire that would never stack up against his love for Laila. But *man*, with that first touch on his shoulder, meant only in comfort, Danni had knocked him for six in a way Laila never had.

Was it possible that, blinded by what he'd thought was real love for Laila, he'd been ignoring something incredible he could have had with Danni? All these years, thinking something was wrong with him, that only lightweight girls returned his desire, while the kind of woman he really wanted—intelligent, sensitive, focussed and strong, never wanted him…

Now his desire was being fulfilled by a woman who not only had all those qualities in spades, but was returning kiss for kiss. Her delicate roundness was lying flush against him, her throat made eager sounds…and he felt as if he were flying. The simple act of kissing—and he'd done a lot of it in the past three years, among other things—had never felt so amazing, so intense.

Why that suddenly brought everything back to him, he didn't know. One moment he felt as if he were captain of Starship Danielle, the next he was putting her down, staggering back and staring at her as if—as if—

Damned if he knew what. Damned if he knew anything at this point.

Within a moment, he regretted his panic-inspired reaction, because Danni had gone from soft, flushed and starry-eyed to having more defences than a hedgehog. Her mouth, dark in the night but he knew was rosy and flushed from his kiss, opened to say something stinging— and he couldn't think of a thing to say to stop her this time.

"Don't tell me—'it's not you, it's me,'" she

said, her tone flippant. Her hands were on her hips, her chin up, ready to do battle.

The trouble was he'd dumped himself on earth from the stratosphere too fast; he couldn't think beyond what had made him panic in the first place. "I don't know who I am." He half turned from her. "My father isn't my father, either. Nobody is who I thought they were—and I'm not anything I thought I was. I have to know the truth."

The sarcasm wiped from her face. When she spoke, the warm, half-laughing ruefulness reached inside his soul, into the pain and softening it. "That's just typical of you, Haskell, you know that? You can put me in the wrong so fast my head spins."

Ridiculously relieved that he'd somehow said the right thing with her for once, he grinned. "Well, you just made my head spin, so we're even."

In the moonlight, he could see her blush.

"I still want you, Danni." He could hear the huskiness in his voice. "But I've got no idea where even I'm going from here, so I can't say where *we* would go."

"I know where you're going. To your parents' house," she said, taking his hand. Her face was very gentle now. "From there—" she shrugged "—I never expected promises. We indulged ourselves for a few minutes, and it was pretty nice. But you have things you have to sort out, and I'm along for the ride while I work out my future. So let's get back to…no, let's *become* friends, Jim Haskell." With a lifted chin and a smile of promised camaraderie, she shook the hand she held.

Not for long, though. Jim released her hand so fast she stumbled back over one of the tree roots, staring at him in shock.

No way!

He could see the danger signs plastered, posted and splashed all over whatever this was with Danni. After that life-changing kiss, she was saying she hadn't wanted anything from him beyond the moment.

Liar. *Liar!*

Danni Morrison was not about to become another woman in the life of Jim Haskell, Woman's Best Friend!

Without warning, everything that had happened to him tonight—or maybe all his *life*—took its toll. Nothing would ever be the same again—and happy-go-lucky, roll-with-the-punches Jim Haskell disappeared. Pure, unadulterated fury flooded through him, all of it currently aimed at the woman trying not to land on her butt between tree roots and powdery red earth.

She'd never called him a friend before—he sure as hell wasn't going to let her get away with that kind of cowardice now. He'd become Danni's *friend* when the equator froze over. The woman was always geared for battle—he'd see how she handled it when someone took up the gauntlet.

Without warning he grabbed her hand. "Come on, let's hit the road," he snarled.

"Jim, what are you *doing*?" she cried as he all but dragged her into the restaurant and snatched up her bag.

"You coming?" he challenged her when, clearly embarrassed by everyone's laughter and knowing grins, she began to pull back, trying to get him to release her hand. "Are you keeping your word, or will you keep lying to me like you just did? Are you going to turn coward and bail because someone finally called your bluff after all these years?"

That was all he needed to say. Her chin lifted, her nostrils flared and she looked at him as if she hated his guts, but she said, "Don't bother turning the tables on me with my own sarcasm,

Haskell. I've done years more psychology than you'll ever know."

"Good, then you can psychoanalyse me on the road, can't you?"

"Or ditch you on it!"

"Yeah, go for it." With deliberate patronage, he patted her on the head. "You handle the verbal attacks. Let's see you get physical again." He grinned down at her. "I dare you."

The entire table of their mutual friends burst into stunned laughter. Laila was blinking, laughing with the others, but clearly flabbergasted. Her best friend—everyone's best friend, sweet and patient, giving Jimmy Haskell had shown his darker side for the first time, not backing down an inch, and none of them knew why.

Damned if he knew why, either. Who would have guessed *Danni* of all people had the power to bring out the tiger in him? Jim himself hadn't dreamed of it until a few minutes ago. But he'd had enough of losing to the women he really wanted.

He didn't question why he really wanted Danni—he only knew he did. And he would *not* take her offer of *friendship* lying down. This time he'd fight, right to the finish.

She *wanted* him, damn it—and he'd force her to come out of wherever she was hiding, make her come to him, to touch him. He'd make her purr for him again....

It seemed he'd knocked out this particular little champ, at least for the moment. Danni's delectable mouth remained closed, but sparks of fury told Jim the bell for the next round was about to ring—as soon as they were alone.

He kissed Laila's cheek. "Congrats, babe. Got to go. I'll call you, okay? Love you."

"You okay, Jimmy?" she whispered.

About to reassure his best friend, he remembered Danni's words about lying to Laila and making her more worried. "No, but I will be. With a little help from my new *friend*." He flicked a deliberate, knowing grin at Danni, whose tight mouth and paleness around distended nostrils told him that *friendship* was the last thing on her mind when it came to him.

Good, he thought in intense satisfaction. He'd rather keep her in a constant passion, even if it was pure fury, than ever receive another offer of friendship from her.

He was going to keep it that way from now on. Bringing Danni's passion to life was worth the price he'd pay later, no matter what kind of passion it was.

And for once, he was looking forward to the battle.

CHAPTER THREE

As HE DRAGGED HER OUT the door, the last
thing Danni saw was her best friend's face.
Laila was gaping at Jim as if she'd never seen
him before.

Or she'd never seen him in this state.

So he'd loved Laila all those years, but she'd
never brought out the caveman in him? A
wave of raw, hot pleasure swept through her.
Fascinating…

With a little smile she was careful to hide, she
snapped back at Jim, "No need to beat me over
the head with your club. You can let go. I already
said I was coming with you."

He shot a dark look at her. "Better leave your
car where it won't get stolen or towed. We'll be
gone at least a week."

"Good idea. My former landlady wouldn't
mind garaging it for a few days."

"Let's go then." Finally he let go of her hand.

She rubbed it. "I think you cut off my circulation."

The Jim of an hour before would immediately have backed down, apologised. *This* Jim lifted a brow. "I think you liked it."

He was right, but no way was she going to show him that. "Can I have my bag, please? A bit hard to drive without my licence or keys."

He tossed it over without a word, before he got into his gorgeous Range Rover—it was a couple of years old, but a definite up-scaling from the half-dead old Valiant of his student days—firing it up hard.

She spent the drive to Mrs. Woodward's boarding house watching him follow her there, and trying to work out what she'd done to turn the official World's Nicest Guy into this challenging stranger. She thought she'd been sweeter and kinder to him than she'd ever been with a man in her life.

With a little frown, she gave it up. Whatever she'd done, she'd either repeat the offence and evoke the same reaction in him, or he'd tell her.

Probably the former, she admitted to herself, grinning—and she'd do it again gladly.

Whatever she'd done, at least it had wiped the confused despair from his eyes...

She could have walked from the Jim she'd known, and become his friend if he'd needed it. Though it wouldn't have been easy, after that *awesome* kiss. The man packed a sensual punch she'd never known before. Offering plain friendship, uncomplicated by the desire clawing through her, had been much harder than she'd expected it to be.

She'd never found it hard to walk away from any man before. But from the moment he'd let her fall back into the tree she'd known letting go wasn't going to be the easy option. The old, sunny Jim had always been gorgeous to her, but this new man intrigued her in a way everybody's best friend Jim never could have. The unashamed hot wanting, raw anger, strong principles and picking up her every challenge without fear lifted plain, old-fashioned lust that didn't have to go anywhere, to a fascination she couldn't deny.

In half an hour the tabby cat had become a stalking lion. There were depths to Jim she'd never dreamed existed. At least she wouldn't need to worry that she'd have to sit beside an emotional basketcase all the way to Goodoona, the outback town where his family lived. Jim was a survivor—just as she was.

Once she'd made the arrangements with Mrs. Woodward, she parked her car safely and climbed into the Range Rover beside him. "I'm going to need my clothes, and to check out of the hotel." She named the place.

He revved up the four-wheel drive necessary for his line of work and locale, and headed toward the hotel. "I'm staying in the place next door. I'll get my stuff and check out while you do the same."

They were on the road within half an hour, heading north out of the university town toward the outback.

"We won't have streetlights for long. Watch out for kangaroos," she reminded him when the silence became uncomfortable…and she began to think of their last silence.

He sent her a withering glance. "I grew up in the outback. Why do you think I've got the roll bars?"

She shrugged. "Just making sure. I don't want to become another Rebecca." One of their former classmates had swerved off the road to avoid hitting a kangaroo, hit a tree head-on instead and was lucky to be alive. Her new life in a wheelchair gave Rebecca massive challenges in her veterinary work. She'd graduated a year after everyone else, thanks to six months on her back and another six or more in physical therapy.

He gave her a sideways look while still watching the road. "I'm sure *Rebecca* didn't want to become a Rebecca."

"I didn't mean it like that." In fact, she was close friends with Rebecca. Her all-female practice in Sydney was one of the two job offers Danni was contemplating. At least she'd be safe from the unwanted male attention her little-girl-lost looks seemed to draw to her.

He shrugged. "Then you should think before you speak."

She clenched her fists in the darkness. "I'm not stupid. I get the picture. How have I become pond scum in the last half hour? I made you angry somehow. So tell me what I did, or get over it. Otherwise I'll be tempted to bail right here and now, and walk back to Bathurst."

He frowned hard. "Bail if you want, Danni. No one's forcing you to come. If you've changed your mind I'll drive you back now."

She sighed loudly. "I didn't say I wanted to bail. I just want to know what's going on."

Silence for a moment. "How about I got the shock of my life tonight and I'm trying to come to terms with it? You know, not everything is about you."

His family.

She tapped her fingernails on the dashboard, feeling small and stupid, and more than a bit self-centred. "Of course not. I'm sorry, Jim."

He flashed a grin at her, so big she could see the gleam of his teeth in the half dark of the street-lights. "Danni Morrison's apologised to me twice in one night. The world must be coming to an end."

Despite wanting to keep up her martyr's position, she caught herself laughing. "Yeah, it must be. I'm apologising, and Jim Haskell's found his temper. If we don't watch out you'll become a regular caveman, and I'll end up like one of the Stepford Wives."

He chuckled. "I don't think there's much danger of either happening for long."

A shame, really… The caveman look is pretty sexy on you.

She had no idea she'd said it out loud until the truck swerved, before he righted it.

Holding onto the balancing handles on the door, she cried, "Watch it, Haskell. I'm not ready to die yet!"

"Then don't say things like that to a man when he's driving." But he was laughing—and he didn't complete her humiliation by commenting further on her unconscious verbal blooper. "And for the record, Danni, I don't think becoming Miss Sweetness and Light would do a thing for you."

She lifted a brow. "So you need to change, but I don't?" she taunted, to keep up the banter, to see how far he'd go with it—and to keep him awake. It was already late.

His face darkened. "I think change is being forced on me whether I like it or not."

Without warning, her throat thickened to a hard ache, but she forced it down. She hadn't cried since she was eight years old, and she wasn't about to start now. To distract him—or maybe because she wanted to—she said huskily, "For the record, Haskell, I thought you were pretty sexy long before the caveman emerged."

This time the silence was charged with unseen fire. "You say that again, Danni, and I'll toss your *friendship* offer out the door," he growled. "A man has his limits."

She felt the heat fill her entire body. Was that what she wanted? *Wasn't* it what she wanted—to be in his arms again, feeling so glorious, feminine and alive as she never had with any man?

Is that what I want—to have a fling with a man who, as honest and giving as he is, will only walk away in the end? I'm not enough for any man.

And Jim had lost enough. The last thing he ought to do now was start a relationship with a woman who knew nothing about love and commitment and happy-ever-after.

Coward. You're making excuses because you're afraid. Yet it was as much truth as lie. She had no clue where she wanted to go from here—and he hadn't said a word about what he wanted, beyond the obvious.

Swallowing down the urge to blurt out what she wanted, she murmured instead, "Mea culpa. Bad timing."

He nodded, his face tight.

Her phone rang—the clashing sound she'd put on to warn her one of her parents was calling. She glanced at Jim. "I'm sorry for whatever you're about to hear.

"Hello," she answered quietly.

"Danielle," the anxious voice of her mother came down the line. Her mother always sounded like a fluttering bird caught in a trap, except when she was talking to her husband. "Was it a nice night for Laila?"

"It was lovely, Mum. Laila made honours. She'll be setting up a practice once the new baby's crawling."

She felt Jim's glance touch her for a moment. It wasn't about Laila, she knew that. He and Laila were still very close, so he'd have heard all the news about her plans to open a practice in a year's time. So he must be reacting to the tightness of her voice. Wondering whether it was talking of Laila that had her so tense, or talking to her mother.

"Ally must be so big now!"

She started at her mother's voice. "Yes, she was running around the hall all day, and the restaurant tonight. Nobody can hold her for long. Just like her mother. She looks more like Jake, though."

"You must tell them to come see me before they head to Queensland, or maybe after the baby's born. It doesn't look as though I'll be a grandmother any time soon. I'd like to hold a baby again."

Her mother didn't know how to tease. She'd spoken blunt truth…but it would take a miracle for Danni to become a mother.

A mother. Pain slashed through her. As if *she'd* ever have a baby, with her lack of nurturing skills. All she knew was how to fight, and she'd never put a child through the constant battles she'd lived all her life. "I'll tell them."

"When are you coming home to see us, Danielle? You haven't been home in almost two months."

"I know." Ever since the last episode, Danni didn't respond to her parents' guilt trips. That house hadn't been *home* to her for a very long time. "I'm busy. I'll come when I can."

"What are you doing now?" her mother asked eagerly. "I know you're between jobs. If Laila's going home to Burrabilla, you can—"

"How do you know I'm between jobs?"

The sharp tone stopped her mother halfway through her sentence. "You didn't answer your phone for a few days, so I called your practice. They said you left a few weeks ago."

She refused to respond to the reproach in her mother's tone. "I've told you before, Mum—don't call me at work unless it's an emergency."

"What else could I do, when you weren't answering your phone?"

Realise I need space from you, and back off for a few days!

"Danielle!"

Her mother's gasp told her she'd done it again. Tonight must be the night she said all the things that, until now, she'd only thought. But no matter how much she wanted to, she couldn't back down. "I don't want to hurt you, Mum, but if I say sorry now, you'll only use it as a weapon against me from now on." *And for the next thirty years, like you do with Dad.*

It was bad enough being their referee. She'd spent her whole life avoiding giving her mother reasons to punish *her,* the way Mum punished Dad. The perfect child, always doing the right thing…and they'd been so proud of her. So when the strain had become too much, she'd simply moved out. It wasn't so hard being nice in a few conversations every day, and monthly or so visits.

"I am your *mother,* Danielle," her mother said now, voice shaking.

Danni sighed, rubbing her forehead as the beginnings of a tension headache began. She'd hurt her mum. "I know that, and I love you. But you don't do anything apart from your job but keep house, play solitaire and talk to me. You need to get out of the house, find friends—get a life beyond me." *And being nasty to and about Dad…*

"Your father and I both want you to come home to see us."

Danni knew the inflexible tone—her mother had reached her limits and was reasserting authority. "I can't. A—a friend needs me. I'm going home with him for a few days."

"Him?" The tone was infused with sudden life. The hope for grandchildren was the one thing that kept both parents going.

"Yes. Jim Haskell. Remember him? Laila's other best friend?" She slid an apologetic glance at Jim, who appeared to be concentrating on the deep darkness of the unlit country road and the song from the CD player, singing along softly.

"The tall, handsome one with the curly hair?"

Danni bit her lip over a grin. "Yes, Mum, the tall, handsome one with the curly hair—and he's sitting right beside me," she said in a mock-long-suffering tone.

Judging by the sudden grin flashing across his face, he'd heard her deliberate repetition.

"I always liked that boy," her mother said, almost quaking in happiness at hearing about a man in Danni's life; but at this point, she'd have liked Attila the Hun if Danni brought him home and said he'd be the father of her grandchildren. "So good-looking, and so kind to everyone."

"I'll tell him you said so."

Her mother gave a small, girlish giggle. "Bring him home for a visit when you come back. What does he like to eat?"

"If he has time, I'll bring him. He runs his own practice, a few hundred kilometres northwest of Bathurst. He eats meat, and drinks coffee and beer," she replied dryly. She'd often had to bite her tongue against a protest about Jim's protein overdoses. "He needs more vegetables and fruit in his diet, and definitely more water."

Jim began singing very loudly.

She bit her lip again, trying not to laugh.

"Are you two…?"

Danni knew her mother would only keep probing if she refused to answer the delicate half question, or she'd believe there was more between them than there was—and she had a million-mile radar against evasions or lies. "I don't know yet."

"I always thought you liked him."

The gentle, smug tone startled her into asking, "You did?"

"It was the way you *wouldn't* look at him, and you were always so sarcastic about his feelings for Laila." Her mother giggled again. "I gather he's over her now."

"I couldn't tell you," she mumbled. The reminder set off a small, sharp ache in her belly. The thought that he'd kissed her like that, still loving Laila…

That she could end up a substitute for the real woman he loved, as Mum had always been for Dad…

What *was* she doing here with him? How could he possibly want her beside him now?

"I have to go, Mum." She didn't bother asking her mother to pass on her love to Dad. She knew it wouldn't be passed. "I need to keep Jim focussed on the road."

"Wait, Danielle—your father wants to speak with you. I'll put him on. George!"

The information, and the calling of her father's name, startled Danni. Since when had her parents talked to each other long enough to know what the other wanted?

She didn't want to think about it; she'd thought about her parents' problems enough for a lifetime. Frowning, she waited until her father took up the phone.

She went through the same questions with her father, the same probing on her life and when she'd be home, that she had just gone through with her mum. Dad, less inflexible than Mum, added another apology for his behaviour during her last visit, and an anxious reassurance that it would *never* happen again.

Awkward, unsure, Danni accepted the apology, not believing a word of it. How could she? They'd had her in their mid-thirties; both were in their sixties now, and they'd always been the same in her living memory. If they could change, she'd never seen a sign of it.

She closed the phone with a sense of fatality, waiting for words of gentle probing or stilted silence; but Jim kept singing as if nothing had happened. Giving her the choice of whether to open the conversation or keep her private things private.

Warmth rushed through her at the respect implied by his actions. Even in silence, this man could bring her to life.

"I'm sorry about that," she offered eventually. "A man anywhere in my life is such an outstanding event my parents can't help hoping it means something."

He flashed a quick grin at her. "Why are you apologising? I learned that your parents like me, they think I'm a good-looking guy and they want you to bring me home. And you didn't say 'no' to whether we're together or not," he added, laughing when her jaw dropped, wondering how on earth he knew that. "It's a pretty good start."

"Start?" she asked, her tummy doing a sudden series of flip-flops.

With a gentle swerve he pulled off to the rough red earth of the roadside, unclipped his seat belt and turned to her. His gaze was intense on her eyes, dropping to her mouth and back. "Look, I don't know what this is, and right now I don't care. I don't care if we're opposites, or if it's bad timing. I won't back down this time, Danni. I won't give up what I want."

"There is no *us*. We're not together," she whispered, forcing the words. "This is just a short-term thing. It's just—just lust."

"Uh-huh." He didn't seem to be listening; his gaze dropped to her mouth.

Her heart was racing, her breathing uneven as her heart and body fought her will. She knew what was right for her, for Jim, but it was fighting this crazy thing between them. Raw *wanting* was drowning her normal sarcasm she used to hide her fears. It was too much; they'd gone from a brief memory to *this* at the speed of a Learjet, and she was off-kilter, unable to control her reactions. Or the flashing of fever inside her whenever he looked at her like that, or told her what he wanted.

"I'm waiting." His eyes like a summer's night on her; mouth bare inches from hers.

A hot shiver raced down her spine.

She didn't dare question the joy screaming inside her, or what it meant, that she'd wanted him far longer than the two years since their graduation day. She'd unbuckled her belt before she knew she was reaching for him.

How he'd done it so fast she didn't know, but he'd pulled his seat right back and down, and pulled her onto him. "About time, woman," he growled as he lifted her face. No tender words, no preliminaries—he kissed her with all the hunger she felt, and it was beautiful.

No slow, exploratory kiss this time. With a cry

muffled by his mouth, she landed on him, loving the feel of him all along the length of her. Her hands, aching and eager, explored his warm skin, the curly hair, his rough jaw. His mouth left hers, and she moaned in deprivation; but the kisses on her jaw and down her throat were sensual, confident, his hands caressing her back and waist making her hunger for more.

The kiss she'd waited for all her life.

No longer a freak of a girl who wondered why the boys at school bored her. No longer the young woman using sarcasm as a shield against anyone coming too close, and seeing that her abnormal home life had infected her body and she wasn't normal, couldn't respond. She'd tried kissing men who'd attracted her in the past, had tried dating to change the missing part inside herself—but she'd only ever felt the cheated wish that she could experience the excitement and passion the other girls whispered about in the change rooms.

She'd felt little to nothing with any man, until the day Laila's other best friend had wrapped an arm around her, kissed her with lingering sweetness and said to an over-familiar stranger, *G'day, sir. I'm Danni's boyfriend…*

The passion she'd felt with his first touch two years ago, his too-brief kiss, wasn't mere excitement: it was the aching pain of all her years of missed womanhood slamming into her body at once. And when he'd walked away from her, it had devastated her. Denial had been her only option.

Anything was better than the truth.

But two years in Europe had done nothing to dim what he'd done to her. None of the men she'd met had the power to make her forget him.

And now she was here in his arms, and it felt as if he was showing her a vision of joy she'd never seen before. Locked away from sunlight too many years, lost in the darkness of her own cynicism, Jim had flown her to the stratosphere in one night, showing her sweetness, blinding light and beauty.

I won't give up what I want.

Now at last he was seeing her, touching her, saying the things she'd waited years to hear from him.

Yes, she admitted in hazy delight, finally willing to end the decade or more of denial. *I want him, I always wanted him, and it drove me crazy that he couldn't see me!*

If she was handing over her prized control to

him, if she'd lost the game she'd played the past fourteen years, with Jim she felt safe—better than safe; this was exquisite surrender.

Was losing so bad, when it meant having this man in her arms?

"I love your hair," he murmured as she arched her head back to take a kiss at the base of her throat, and her waist-length hair trailed across his hands and shoulders. "Always such a fighter—but you always leave your hair out, soft and feminine." He let a handful slide through his hand. "Like silk…like *you*. There's so much strength inside you, but you're still proud to be the beautiful woman you are."

She felt the quiver run right through her. Jim made her *feel* like a beautiful woman—he made her feel that, in his eyes, to be a beautiful woman was neither to be weak nor dominated, but to hold power over a man she'd never dreamed of before.

She couldn't say any of it—she had no experience with sweet words—so she lifted his face from her throat and kissed him again, deep and hot and sweet. His aroused body beneath hers wasn't the threat of male domination and feeling of suffocating fear she'd always known with men before, but choice, power, beauty—because it was Jim.

And with every kiss, she was making memories to store. Sooner or later, he would realise she wasn't enough for him, that what this was wouldn't last beyond a few weeks, and he'd leave her life again.

"You're sad," he murmured against her mouth. "What is it, Danni-girl?"

She pulled back, startled that he'd read her so easily. Not even Laila, or her parents, had ever been able to reach inside her walls to *feel* her deepest-hidden emotions this way.

He smiled at her, lazy, sleepy. "You were with me, but somewhere in the kiss, I felt like I lost you."

It startled her over again. Not only had he read her, he wasn't suffering the shallow male pride that made them all so offended when she wasn't lost in their touch. Yet still she bit her lip, not sure how to answer him.

He touched her face. "Family stuff?"

Attempting a brave smile, she nodded. She wasn't lying. It was family—in a way. She was who she was. A product of her strange, cold family, as much as he was a product of his open-hearted, loving and trustworthy family.

Except that they'd lied to him all his life.

It didn't matter, not for them, anyway. He was what he was, and she was *this*. It couldn't happen, whatever he thought…at least, not for long.

"We should go," she whispered—but she didn't move. Couldn't move.

His gaze grew hooded with sensuality. "Not yet. Come here."

Wanting nothing more than that, she murmured, "This isn't smart. There's too much history, and too much going on right now…for this to go anywhere, or last beyond what we're doing now."

Every word seemed forced from a reluctant throat—and it was as much lie as truth. Every word she forced her mouth to speak had done battle with her body's screaming need.

For Jim's sake.

It seemed he'd read her internal struggle, for he smiled again, slow, sensual. "Is that what you want?" His mouth—that full, lush mouth—touched hers as he spoke.

She heard a soft whimper, and was amazed it came from her throat. "Jim," she whispered, leaning down to kiss him again, and then again. He wound a hand through her hair, caressed her neck and throat with the soft strands as he kissed her back, deep and gentle.

Giving her the choice to stay, or to move.

Does he know? She wondered, lost again in the rush of exquisite sensations he roused in her with a word, a touch. *Can he understand that the power he gives me traps me? When he gets tired of all my walls and smart cracks, will I be trapped for the rest of my life, wanting what I can't have? The same way I've been trapped inside wanting him for so long?*

Trapped longing turned to hate—as my mother is with my father? Was this how she felt the night she conceived me...the only night my father ever wanted or liked her?

"This is going to happen for us, Danni-girl," he murmured against her mouth. "I know you're trying to fight it—" he grinned at her as she gasped again "—I could feel you trying to marshal up your arguments even while you were kissing me." He lifted her from his hard, ready body, and raised the seat so she was in his lap.

Irritable with the way he could read her, unable to *think* with him so close to her—keeping her aroused just by being there—she wriggled back, but he held her against him. "I think it's easier to talk if I'm in my own seat."

His grin didn't abate. "Hard to think, is it?" he

murmured and moved against her, surrounding her with his warmth and strength.

She *hated* the way he could make her so breathless, so brainless with a single movement!

Unwilling to lie to him, unable to answer with truth, she drew in a shaking breath and pushed against him. She felt the most absurd rush of disappointment when he let her go—knowing he gave her power, but could take control back with ease: not with physical power or crude sarcasm, but with a smile, a touch, or his compelling honesty.

How could she be so angry, so filled with wanting and yet *respect* him so much at the same time?

She scrambled over to the passenger's seat, well aware of her lack of dignity—but he didn't laugh or even smile at it. "Ready?" he asked gravely, when she'd rearranged her skirt, pulled down her tank top and smoothed her hair.

She had so many thoughts jumbling around in her head she barely knew where to start, so she was even more surprised than he when she said, out of nowhere, "Did you come to graduation today, thinking you could still be in love with Laila?"

He flinched. It was answer enough.

She took a few breaths to clear her head. "My father lost the love of his life, you know. He slept with my mother on the rebound, and got her pregnant with me. So he did the right thing by her, and by me…and I've spent my entire life wishing he'd done a runner. Maybe then Mum would have found someone to make her happy. Then she wouldn't hate him so much for never even trying to love her. She always knew she was a replacement—and while I know how much he loves me, I also wonder if he'd had a child by that other woman, would he have even bothered with me?"

She couldn't look at him as she finished baring her soul, telling a truth she'd never told anyone. Knowing she didn't have to say any more. Jim was smart; he'd connect the dots…but whether he'd understand or become furious, she had no idea.

She waited for him to speak, and waited, until she started scrambling around in her mind for something else to say.

She started when she felt him take her hand in his, softly caressing the back. "It's not what you think, Danni. I wondered, that's all—then I came, saw Laila and was happy for her. That's all. It was gone. If it wasn't, I would never have kissed you."

She felt her brows lift. "You've kissed a lot of girls in the past few years, or so I hear."

He grinned at her. "Been keeping count, have we?"

She frowned at him. "This is serious, Jim. Why am I any different to those girls?"

The grin faded. "Because you are. I can't tell you why. You just are." He sighed and shrugged. "I don't know what to tell you, Danni…tonight's been a crazy night. I don't know what I think or feel about anything."

"I understand that," she murmured, wishing she'd never started the conversation. Jim was too honest to hide from her, and whatever he was about to say would hurt.

"I didn't even know I wanted you so badly until tonight. I thought…" he sighed.

Her heart jerked. *Laila.* Always Laila…

"Until tonight I wondered, you know? It was so intense that day. Now, everything's changing on me, and you're part of it. Again. Just like last time."

He'd been talking about *her?* He *remembered* how her touch had felt to him? Her gaze flew to his, startled, frightened and so unsure.

He nodded. "Why do you think I took off so

fast? I was still getting over Laila then. I didn't want anything but casual things." His eyes were shadowed in the darkness, but she could feel the intensity coming from him in waves. "I don't know what's going on here, Danni, but I could never treat you like that." He didn't mention her father; he didn't have to. They both knew. "All I know right now is that I have a lot to work out in my life—and you're part of the confusion."

"A small part compared to everything else," she suggested, trying to smile but failing.

"No, damn it. I was feeling the confusion before—" He sighed and shook his head. "You saw it, Danni. Don't pretend you didn't. You're a woman—you know when a man can't take his eyes off you. My date took off because I was looking at you all night. This thing between us…"

Looking back at her lap, she mumbled, "I'm sure my father was like that with my mother—at least for one night."

"Danni—"

"No, Jim, don't. I know you're confused, and you want someone beside you through your ordeal—and the fact that we have a thing for each other makes it all convenient for you. I'm a good distraction, a way for you to bury the pain you don't want to deal with yet."

Jim laughed, but it wasn't sweet. "I doubt any man would call you convenient…and I haven't treated you that way. Though you are one hell of a distraction," he added wryly.

"Fine, then tell me now—if Laila was single, if Jake had never come into the picture, would I still be sitting here?" she challenged him.

Again, the silence spoke for itself. She risked a glance up at him. The low-slung moon threw soft light on his face. He looked lost inside turbulent confusion. "Do you want me to take guesses here, Danni? Or lie to you?"

"No," she sighed. "Let's not talk of anything beyond now. Not until your life's sorted out and you know what you want."

"Do you know what *you* want?" But it wasn't shot at her; it was spoken with the exhaustion of a man who'd been through the emotional wringer.

"No, I don't," she admitted. "Look, I'll stand beside you through what you have to do, Jim." She spoke very quietly. "I'll be here until you don't need a—a friend. I won't let you down. But don't use me to forget your family problems."

"So you'll give me your patronising kindness,

because it makes you feel strong, right? But if I want something deeper, you'll scuttle for cover, just as you always do." His face was grim and cold as he withered her shield under the light of plain honesty. "Heaven forbid you allow yourself to feel normal human emotion, or actually take a risk for once. You want to be with me beyond tonight, Danni," he snarled. "You want more than a few kisses, too. Admit it, at least to yourself!"

She flushed in the darkness, glad he couldn't see it. "Yes," she said, holding onto her temper with a thinning thread. "I do want you. That's too rare an event for me to be a one-night thing. But you have too much going on in your life. I don't want to be your transition woman between Laila and the next woman you fall in love with."

"Fine, I'll stay away from you until you come to me." His voice was harsh and cold. He released her hand and turned from her. "And you will, Danni. Because *using you* implies you were helpless in this—that you didn't come on to me tonight as much as I did you, when we both know you did. This thing is crazy, it might have come out of nowhere for both of us—but it's mutual. Be honest with yourself, if not with me."

Be honest with yourself. It was the most ironic of times—just as it seemed she'd succeeded in pushing him away—to realise how much this man, *only this man,* meant to her. It was unfair, but nobody gave you a contract with your birth certificate saying life would be fair.

For the first time in her life she truly, deeply wanted a man—she wanted Jim. But until he'd sorted out his family problems, and his feelings for the best friend they both shared—someone neither of them would ever cut out of their lives or hearts—she had to take control.

The truth is, I'm protecting myself…even from a man as honest as Jim.

She hated the weakness the admission implied, but it was true. Just as her mother never competed with her dad's first love, she knew she could never live up to the kind of woman Laila was. She could only ever be a replacement, a second-best lover for a few days, weeks or months—and when he walked away again, it would destroy her.

She clenched her hands together in her lap. "I think we should go."

"Put on your seat belt." His voice was tight and hard. "Go to sleep. I'll wake you when it's your shift to drive. We have nine hours to go." He reached into the back and tossed her a light blanket and a pillow.

Miserable, she turned on her side away from him and huddled into the pillow, wishing she was anywhere but here.

CHAPTER FOUR

Read

DANNI DIDN'T MOVE OR CHANGE rhythm in her breathing to show she was awake, even though she should have offered to take over the driving an hour ago.

Facing Jim was just too hard.

What he'd said about his life changing was true—what he didn't realise was that in a single hour, *hers* too had changed, irrevocably. He'd tossed out her best defence: her years of denial, of her belief in her strength. *She* didn't need a man to complete her life. She didn't need anyone.

She'd gone to the graduation with only one thing in mind, besides sharing Laila's joy: she wanted to test her strength in seeing him again. Two years of distance and touring the world should surely have cured her of the *thing* she had for him. She'd refused to dignify it with a name.

But he'd forced her out of hiding, made her tell him how she felt without even seducing her first. He'd done it based only on the depth of her aching for him. *I want you, all right? I want to be with you.*

If only he knew. *Want* seemed a pitiful way to describe the craving, the hunger…

Could she go back now? Could she forget? That one brushing of her lips had lingered in her mind and body for two years. The kisses tonight had hit her like a beautiful explosion, destroying a decade of self-delusion.

She *was* a normal woman…but was she a *one-man* woman? The thought terrified her.

So what? Her mind shot back, in immediate denial. *It's still just desire, lust, whatever. I'm nothing like Laila. This will only last a few days. I can survive that. I refuse to be just a time-filler for him while he's between women he loves.*

Laila wasn't just pretty; she had that invisible *something* that made them both adore her, that giving wisdom, the loving, constant need for them both…

That's why he always loved her. Jim has to be needed—and I can't stand to lower my defences. I make one admission of how I feel about him, and I want to bolt.

They were complete opposites, she and Jim. She was compulsively organized; he was cheerful in his mess. She cared for her health; he downed beer, coffee and meat with complete disregard for the cholesterol levels beckoning in his future. He was a country boy; she was a city girl.

He was part of a happy family, and she—

And all of that was why she was safe: the more he saw her defences and her sarcasm, the more he'd want to run. He'd never want more than these days together. So she'd take what she could get with him while it lasted, which wouldn't be long, given her track record in turning men off, and smile and wave goodbye when it ended. She could do that.

Right now, though, it wasn't Jim who had to give to her, or worry about her hurt. Jim's life had disintegrated, and for the first time in her life she had to put her barriers to one side, and be the person he needed.

She knew, none better, that it should have been Laila here with him now; she was a pitiful replacement who didn't have a clue how to give him what he needed.

Laila…

Of course! She might not *be* Laila, but she'd give her best imitation of the friend Jim needed with him now.

For Jim's sake.

How the hell did a man's life explode in every possible direction in a single night?

Jim kept driving long after he knew he'd hit exhaustion levels—the adrenaline coursing through his system wouldn't let him rest. Danni might as well get some sleep; he had too many thoughts and emotions tumbling round in his head.

But he knew she was awake. He could hear the tiny hitch in her breathing; he could feel her stillness without relaxing. She didn't want him to know she was awake.

He'd give her space until she was ready to talk.

Strange, that. He'd never had such a deep instinct with a woman before—and that it had come with a woman he hadn't even known he liked until tonight had thrown him completely off-kilter.

He'd expected that feeling to come with Laila, but it hadn't been there for either of them. He hadn't even known the yearning for human touch could be so deep until tonight.

Why it was Danni for him, he had no idea—just

as he had no clue why he couldn't stop staring at her face, or why her kiss left him reeling with hunger, with wanting more and more.

The sky to the west, vast and clear, unpunctured by buildings and artificial light, became touched with the soft golden-rose of pre-dawn.

They were less than a hundred kilometres from home.

Goodoona. Home and family and peace—

And lies. A lifetime of lies...

"Do you want to talk about it?" Her voice came to him in the darkness, sliding into his consciousness as easily as if she belonged there.

Still, he shrugged. Sharing his feelings with anyone was too new an experience for him to be comfortable with it; accepting her presence here, accepting her comfort earlier was all he could handle right now.

Danni liked it that way, too. She gave on her terms, sure, but she'd rather give than admit she needed anything from anyone. It had always irritated him about her.

Because you're too alike that way.

He frowned. Where had *that* thought come from? No *way* was he like Danni, with all her prickly retorts and her self-protective shells.

"A lot has happened tonight, Jim. You might want to get some of it out before you see your family. Otherwise you might say some things you'll regret later."

The gentle, reasonable voice sent jagged edges of anger through him. Danni, furious, sarcastic and frightened Danni—*wanting, hungering* Danni—yeah, he could handle all she dished out and come back for more. But this new woman beside him sounded like some damn *counsellor* in a session with a patient.

"I'm fine. I know what I'm going to say." *Did he?*

"I don't think so, Jim." Her voice sounded so tender, so understanding. So—*friendly.* "The trauma you've suffered tonight isn't the kind you can overcome in a few hours. You're not Superman, you know—you can share the burden with someone."

"With *you?*" He heard himself jeering, and though he hated hearing the bitterness coming from his mouth, he couldn't seem to stop himself. "Yeah, you're the perfect person to offload to, right? Danni Morrison is known for her kind, giving nature and her wisdom. A regular font of unselfish understanding."

He felt her flinch, and felt a savage shot of satisfaction. She'd made him flinch enough tonight with her questions—it was time the boot reached her foot. "I may not be any of the things you said, but I've been there with my parents—"

"Yeah, it sounded like it before," he snapped, wanting to wound her, to shock her out of this cloak of sweetness and caring she'd pulled over her acidic nature.

Lies, all lies! Just like my damned family!

"You really know how to deal with your parents, don't you?" he kept on, refusing to look at her in case he couldn't stop looking at her, and forgot this fury that preserved him safe. "You know how to fight back, but you haven't got a clue how to be honest. You give them what they want to hear, and slide out of anything you don't want to give. Yeah, sounds like you've got a ton of wisdom to get me through my upcoming ordeal." He made the word *ordeal* flippant, as if he didn't care. He couldn't stand her to see past his attitude to the roiling stomach and shaking hands, the pounding heart. Just as he couldn't stand her patronising words and kind, *sisterly* manner. Damn it—why couldn't she just be honest?

"Feeling any better for attacking me?" she asked quietly.

He almost started with her perception. "Is this Psychology lesson 101 you're passing off on me? Maybe you've got a handy label to put on me while you're at it, and make tonight perfect?"

"If you like." Her voice was less kind, less reasonable now.

Again, satisfaction shot through him. "Go for it, little Freud," he said in his most patronising manner.

"You have many of the classic signs of an enabler."

He was too startled to keep bantering. "A what?"

"An enabler is almost always the oldest child in the family, or the child or partner of addictive personalities, like alcoholics or drug addicts." She spoke in a calm, unemotional tone. "The enabler finds his or her strength in keeping those they love weak and needy. They equate need with love and personal strength." She gave him a short, speculative look. "They don't teach others to fix their problems so they can grow strong—the enabler solves the problems over and over again, because they want another call for help soon."

The words took a minute to sink in, but then a flash of pure fury shot through him. "Did you get a high distinction for that load of psycho-babble in first year? Did you recite it verbatim from your textbook? It sounded like you've been waiting a decade to unleash that wisdom on someone."

"You wouldn't need to attack me if part of you didn't acknowledge the truth, Jim." She lifted her chin and stared him down. "Tell me one time someone asked for help and you didn't give it. Tell me when you weren't hanging around Laila, dealing with her hassles for her, so she never learned to cope with the teasing the rest of us got. She never learned to stand alone with you around."

"Who got Laila her job? Was that enabling her?" he argued, ignoring the tiny voice nagging inside that she was right. He'd seen it with Jake—Jake had hurt Laila, sure; but he'd challenged her, tested her strength and allowed her to find it on her own. He'd allowed the girl to become a woman, simply because he hadn't treated her any other way.

If I'd been Jake, I'd have married her and kept her safe...and Laila wouldn't be the strong, resourceful woman she was now. Jake was good for her.

So he'd made stupid mistakes with Laila—he

hadn't done her any permanent damage, had he? She didn't come crying to him with her problems now; she sorted them out herself.

Because Jake taught her to stand on her own feet. It had nothing to do with me.

"Who arranged Jodie's second and third practicals when she was almost failing, so she could scrape through?" he went on, when her silence spoke for itself. She knew what he was thinking, damn it.

"Did you do that for them, or for yourself?" she asked softly. "Did you feel good about it, and glad *you* had the power to create something from nothing?"

"Dr. Danni," he mocked, even more furious, if that were possible because part of him, the honesty he couldn't submerge, acknowledged the truth in her words. "You should run your own talk show. I didn't know you had it in you to be so perceptive!"

He felt her gaze on him. "Who is it you've spent your life rescuing, Jim? You do it now so naturally for all your friends—even for me two years ago—it's obvious it's become learned behaviour for you. I'd say one of your brothers or sisters is an addictive personality."

"Oh, very good," he muttered savagely,

gripping the wheel so tightly he felt as if his bones would soon snap. "Have you spent the past few years dissecting me, so you can belittle my good deed for you? So then you don't owe me—or is that what the kisses tonight were? Payback to the good boy scout?"

Her voice shook. "I'm trying to help you, as hard as it is for you to accept."

"Would you like to lay me down on a couch and have me tell you about my mother?" he snapped. "Sorry, I only just talked to her for the first time tonight, so I can't tell you much except that she couldn't be bothered keeping me. So I'd appreciate it if you morphed back into the Danni I know—the one who uses IQ and sarcasm as a shell to hide her insecurities and the fear that you're so damn transparent, we all know you're not like the rest of us!"

A shaking hand lifted, then fell. "If I'm abnormal, then you've just joined me. The Jim I thought I knew all these years would never hurt someone to hide the fact that he's terrified of what he's about to hear." Her voice quivered with emotion.

"You don't know me. You never wanted to know me," he growled.

"You're right. I don't know you at all." Her hands folded together in her lap, in a controlled motion, but she was shaking. "I'm sorry I can't be Laila. I know you would have talked to her."

Thwack.

The arrow of shame hit him with unexpected force. He might have beaten her, but at what cost? He dragged in a breath that felt too hot for his lungs to bear. "Danni…"

She turned her face to the side window. "Just pull over. You're exhausted. You shouldn't face your parents in this state. I'll take over until I find a trucker's stop. We could both use breakfast, and some coffee."

Her voice was thick, as if she was fighting tears.

Without another word he pulled over, too *scared* to say another word in case he felt like more of a jerk than he did now.

He climbed out; so did she. He walked around the back of the car; she walked around the front. They climbed back in. She started the car and drove.

All very civilised, so polite. They didn't look at each other, didn't speak until they found the trucker's stop. Then their only words were about food preferences and the best directions to his parents' town. They could have been total strangers.

The lovers of the night had vanished.

The entire family seemed to be waiting for Jim to arrive. The timber house was bursting at the seams with men, women and children wanting to see him. A sea of people flooded from the door the moment the car turned into the muddy driveway.

The forward momentum halted with shocking suddenness when his family, as one, caught sight of Danni in the driver's seat.

No wonder. I don't belong here. I was stupid to think I could help at all. They don't want me here—Jim doesn't even want me here.

It was obvious by the way he'd decimated her that he wasn't interested in sharing himself with her. It was only physical, and now it seemed as if that was over, too. One night was all she'd gotten with him.

Jim muttered something beneath his breath, grabbing her attention. Danni could see what he was thinking: *Did the whole family but me know about my life?*

More than anything, she wanted to reach out to squeeze his hand, to let him know he wasn't alone. Instead, awkward after his attack on her earlier, she sat in silence, waiting for him to tell her what he wanted her to do.

She felt his glance touch her. "They can get a bit overwhelming en masse. I'm related to almost all the town."

A smile hovered around her mouth, but didn't quite form. "You don't need numbers to be overwhelmed." Her parents overwhelmed her constantly.

He unbuckled his seatbelt. "May as well come meet everyone."

Given her cue, she nodded and followed him out of the car.

Danni soon realised what Jim meant by *overwhelming*. Around sixty pairs of eyes staring at her in silence made her feel like a new breed of germ under a microscope. Like a fool she stood there, and allowed them to look. Trying to smile, unsure if she'd managed it.

"This is Danni, a friend of mine from uni days," Jim said in the silence. "These are my…parents, Bob and Claire, my…aunts and uncles—and—and everyone else is related," he added wryly. "You'll meet them all in time."

Danni wondered if she was the only one that

heard the slight stumble before the titles. Surely they all knew the significance? Why were they all *here,* when they must know he wanted to be private with his parents?

The thin, dark woman with a kind face that Danni had seen at every university milestone for Jim through the years rushed to him the moment he spoke. "Kilaa. Kilaa." She hugged him close and sniffed, obviously trying to hold in the emotion.

Jim looked down at his adopted mother, with a curious mixture of deep love and confused betrayal. "It's all right…Mum. It's all right. I'm fine." He patted her back; but he stood at an angle where Danni could see him. His eyes were haunted with deep-hidden anger, grief, loss and a dozen other emotions she couldn't identify.

"No, it isn't all right, Jim. You're not fine with this. Don't lie to them."

It was only when every single person standing around turned to frown at her—even the children—that Danni realised the words had come from her.

Shocked by her runaway mouth she could only stand there, feeling the heat creep up her cheeks and wish she knew how to make time go backward. *That's right, meet the man's family and alienate them.* So typical of her! "I'm—sorry…"

Jim released his mother and stepped into the breach. "Don't apologise when you're right, Danni. I'm not fine." He offered everyone a tired smile. "Guys, I love you all, but can you go away for a few hours? I need to talk to Mum and Dad, alone."

The kids scattered to their own pursuits. From country work experience, Danni knew the blistering summer holidays in tiny outback towns like Goodoona meant taking turns on the tyre swings by the tree-lined river or the local billabong if there was any water in the drought. They'd ride their bikes or skateboards along the rough, unsealed roads and hills if there was no water, or sit in the shade with a Game Boy.

As one, the adults turned their gazes to Jim's parents, and didn't start moving off until both of them nodded. And though she knew that was a cultural courtesy, obeying the wishes of the elders first, it still felt as if Jim's wishes in the matter were less important, Danni thought, frowning in turn. Why was it that such a giving man so often had his needs overlooked by those who loved him?

Jim either hadn't noticed or was used to that

kind of response. He merely waited, smiling in a weariness that looked bone-deep.

When everyone had gone, she touched his arm. Asking without words: *Do you want me to stay with you?*

"Danni, would you like a cup of tea or breakfast before you leave us alone with Jimmy?" his father asked with a confused frown. "It was nice of you to come with him…."

"He was very upset, Mr. Haskell," Danni replied with a straight look. "I was worried about him. Driving this far in shock isn't good. He needed a friend."

"You know what's going on. You know our family business." His mother's statement was flat. Almost an accusation. *You're an outsider.*

Danni turned her gaze on Jim's mother. No apology this time. "He needed a friend, Mrs. Haskell. He didn't want to be alone. Wouldn't you have needed someone at a time like that? Didn't you turn to people who care about you after he called you last night?"

"I stayed within the family." The other woman shifted on her feet and moved the accusing gaze to Jim. "We shouldn't talk about our private business outside like this."

"Or with strangers," his father added with a dark glance at Jim, then Danni. "This is our business, son. No one else's."

The inference was obvious: she was to make herself scarce. They wanted Jim alone and out-numbered, while they projected all their guilt and anger onto him. And Jim would take back the role he was used to. The peacemaker would take the burden, make them feel better about themselves, and they could carry on as normal, while Jim, the victim in all this, would be the one screwed up….

Jim neither moved nor spoke. He didn't look at her.

He expected her to excuse herself and desert him.

She'd regret her cowardice the rest of her life if she left him alone now.

There was only one way to demand her place in this very private conversation, and though her heart pounded and her stomach clenched until it was pain, she grabbed the opportunity before she lost her courage. "Jim had no family to share with last night—but he knew he could tell me." She smiled at them both. "I'm sorry for this unusual introduction to the family, Mr. and

Mrs. Haskell, but Jim asked me to come—to be with him. I'm not just his friend, we're together," she said as she moved to him, rushing the words before she bolted. "I'm not leaving him." She took the final step and threaded her fingers through Jim's. "I have the right to be with him."

His hand closed convulsively over hers—and she couldn't look at him. What if she'd gone too far, said too much? She didn't know a lot about Aboriginal culture, or his family's expectations. What if—

"Danni has the right."

At the strong voice, Danni glanced at him. He was smiling at her with a warm intimacy that stole her breath. He bent and brushed his mouth over hers, soft and lingering. "I want her with me."

She clutched his hand as her knees quivered. Couldn't she control her reaction to him at this very difficult time? *Focus, focus, Danni! He needs you now…*

Her body seemed to have blocked off from good sense—and no wonder. She'd thought it was over…but he wanted her still.

"Fair enough, then. I suppose it's your decision on who hears our personal business,"

Jim's father snapped, breaking into her reverie. "Let's go inside before everyone else knows."

"I think everyone else here already knows— and whether Danni hears it or not is *my* business, Dad," Jim said, harsh and pointed. "It seems to me Danni and I are the only ones in town who don't know *my* business."

Bob Haskell stopped mid-stride and turned to his son, his eyes filled with the same confused betrayal Jim's held. "Let's go inside, Kilaa. We can discuss it in private."

In silence, Jim led Danni into and through the house that was bigger than it had seemed at first—the tacked-on additions led farther and farther back. It was simply furnished, but clean and comfortable, with worn rugs covering the wooden floors. He led her to an extendable dining setting beside the kitchen near the back of the house. The kitchen was bright and neat, with white cupboards and earth-tone bench tops.

"Is this private enough now, Dad?" Jim's voice was so rough it grated. "Or do you have a few more stalling tactics before I learn anything about my life I might need to know?"

Danni closed her eyes and wished for a

moment that she'd taken the coward's way out and left them alone. It seemed to her that Jim would do fine on his own.

"When did everyone find out, Dad? Last night—or have they always known the story? Am I the only one in the family, in the town, who doesn't know my true history and parentage?"

"Kilaa." His mother's voice was full of rebuke. "Don't speak that way to your father!"

Quick as a flash, Jim turned on her. "*Is* he my father, Mum? Is that another secret I didn't know until now?"

Claire Haskell closed her mouth, her eyes filled with pain. "I'll make some tea. Would you like some breakfast, Danni?"

"I'm fine, thanks, Mrs. Haskell," she said, feeling sorry for the poor woman; she obviously wanted something positive to do. "A cup of tea would be nice, though."

"We ate on the road," Jim snapped. "Danni might want tea, but I need answers. Such as, how are your names listed as my parents on my birth certificate? And is my birth date right, or is that another lie?"

The quiet was like a case loaded with explosives: one wrong move and everything would blow apart. Danni had never heard Jim sound so hard, so unforgiving….

"We don't know your exact day of birth, son," Bob said quietly. "Annie didn't tell us, just that you were two weeks old. So we applied for a birth certificate for August 18th."

"Why aren't my real parents' names on the certificate?"

Claire choked back a sob as she rattled the teacups. "She—didn't want to be named. We wanted to be your parents, Kilaa. And the government was still taking kids away then. The police could have taken you from us if they'd known you were their child, not ours, with white grandparents. We didn't want you to—to ever have to—"

Jim's face didn't soften with the revelation that he, too, could have been taken away; he didn't seem to have heard it. "To find out my mother never wanted me? I think I've worked that out. What I want to know is, did she have any other kids she actually kept? Do I have *real* brothers and sisters I haven't met? And who the hell is my real father?"

Claire's sob wasn't choked down this time. "Kilaa…"

Danni jumped to her feet and rushed to help

the other woman. While she didn't question Jim's right to this outburst of anger, Claire was in no condition to handle boiling water. "Please sit down, Mrs. Haskell. I can do this for you."

"Thank you, Danni. Milk please, and two sugars for us all," Claire answered in a thick, teary voice and sat down.

"Black coffee, thanks, Danni," Jim said without looking at her. "I don't like tea."

Both the Haskells blinked. "You don't like tea?" Claire asked, sounding more dazed, if that were possible. "You always drink tea at home. You never said…"

"You made it, I drank it." Jim shrugged. "There's a lot of stuff you don't know about me. And a lot of stuff I don't know about myself."

Bob sighed and touched Jim's hand. "We haven't heard from Annie in at least fifteen years, son. We don't know if she has kids, if she's with your father, or if she even knew who he was. She was a pretty mixed-up kid, you know?"

"We didn't want to know." Tears were flowing freely down Claire's face. "From the moment she put you in my arms, you were our boy, safe with us. In time we forgot you belonged to anyone else."

If she had scripted the words, they couldn't have been better aimed to end his anger and betrayal. Jim's eyes closed for a moment, to come to terms with the shaft of pain lancing through him. He loved the people who'd raised him; he trusted—correction, he *had* trusted them. Until last night, he'd have said his parents were the most honest people he knew.

And hearing their pain, he wanted to erase it for them somehow. More than anything he wanted to say, *I am your son. I do belong to you.* But he couldn't make the words form. He no longer knew who or what he was, and letting his—letting Claire and—oh, *damn it*, he didn't even know how he felt about calling them his mother and father anymore. "Well, Annie didn't forget—so let's start with her. Why do you think she called me after spending thirty years forgetting me?"

He picked up the mug Danni had put in front of him, inhaling the scent of coffee with a sense of familiar relief. He accepted her hands on his shoulders, slowly kneading the muscles that had been knotted since Annie's call last night.

The silent support calmed and soothed him. Danni stood behind him, asking nothing and giving all, and it felt *right*.

The thought of her being his woman fit so naturally, he also accepted it without question. Whether that feeling would last beyond this week, this month, he didn't know. There were too many uncertainties in his life to know where they'd go from here. But Danni was *his,* for however long they lasted.

He leaned his head back against her in silent thanks for her presence before he spoke. "You're her sister. Why do you think Annie called me?"

At his gentler tone, Mum—Claire—*damn it, she is my mother, in every other way that counts*—looked up, with a smile that wavered. "I don't know her, Kilaa. I knew *of* her, and how much it hurt your grandmother when she was taken away. I only met her when she brought you here, and I haven't seen her since." She shrugged. "I can only make a guess."

"Go on," he said quietly.

She frowned. "Kilaa...remember I don't know her. I could be wrong."

"You think she heard I'm a vet with my own practice, and she wants a cut," he said, his tone as flat as his heart felt in having to say it for her.

He didn't need his mother's nod of confirmation. The thought had occurred to him last night, as soon as the first shock had worn off. Annie had asked too many calculated questions, without giving a hint of the emotion expected in a real mother finding her son, talking to her firstborn for the first time.

She didn't want *him*. She wanted something from him. Now he had to find out what it was before she called him again.

Forewarned was forearmed.

CHAPTER FIVE

Read.

AS THE SUN BEGAN TO SET HOURS later, Danni sat on powdery red earth beneath the shade of a ghost gum down the back of the Haskell backyard. Jim needed time with his family.

Though it was almost 8:00 p.m., the heat was still pulsing up from the land in dry, hot waves, shimmering all around her. As deceptive as it was beautiful, for your sweat dried so fast out here you didn't know you were dehydrated until the dizzy spells began.

The outback was as dangerous as it was addictive. She loved coming here, but she always returned to the safety, the anonymity of the city. In a place of over four million people, few knew her business and less cared. Here, everyone knew your business in hours, and they were all in your face, wanting to know what they could do to help.

She turned her head to look in the house. They

were still surrounding him like flies around honey. Just as everyone always had in their uni days. Everybody loved Jim.

Then why hadn't anyone else come out to him that night in the restaurant? She shook her head at the strangeness of human nature. No wonder she tried to avoid people.

Everyone had begun trickling back to the house within three hours of leaving it, the worried look on each face discounting her cynical thought that they wanted to satisfy their curiosity. Every one of them came to Jim first, and hugged him without a word, before moving on to Bob and Claire. Giving reassurance of their love and support, *family* support, in the awkward silence of people who didn't know what to say.

Or maybe it was just an old song sung one too many times. There was barely an Aboriginal family in this state that hadn't been touched by the effects of the Stolen Generations, the children forcibly taken by government authorities over a century. She'd learned about the subject in the Australian History and Politics classes she'd taken to round out her education.

She'd never expected it to touch her life in such a personal way...or that she'd *want* to be involved. But now she was here, this had become more than payback for his kindness to her. This was personal for her. She *wanted* to be here for Jim, to give him the support, the—

I want to be with him, no matter what price I have to pay later.

That was the real truth. She wanted to help him if she could; she wanted to be sure he'd make it though the turbulent waters of family deceit. But more than anything, she wanted to be where Jim was. She'd never felt so strongly about a man before…and she wanted to see—

See if it can last? See if he can feel anything for me besides the obvious desire?

See if I can mean as much to him as Laila does?

She took a long sip on the icy pineapple cordial she'd brought out with her. No—it wasn't Laila that threatened her, not anymore. She knew that if he still felt anything for Laila, he'd have shown it that night in the restaurant. No, that had to be over.

Then what was it—the real reason she was still here?

You want him. It's as simple as that.

But it could never be so simple for her…not

with a man like Jim, who would expect to meet her parents even if this was just a fling. It was a sign of respect he'd show anyone.

It was too frightening. Her parents had never met any man she'd dated—and if they did now, with her approaching thirty, they'd expect him to be the one. The stress of disappointment could trigger an argument—

Yeah, right. It'd be more like war games, the two of them locked in a blame-fest while I die of shame....

She'd always known, in some deep part of her, that Mum's bitter vitriol against Dad was love turned sour, hopes thwarted. Mum had been a friend of the woman Dad had loved, and when her friend had dumped him, she'd allowed herself to be that woman's replacement for a night, a week...and the resulting pregnancy had set her up for thirty years of misery.

Mum got herself pregnant. I refuse to put myself in that position of humiliation!

Laila did, and look how happy she is, an imp in her mind whispered. *She took a massive risk on Jake, and won the man she loved.*

Yeah, so did Mum—and I'm not Laila.

The awful, down-the-sink sound told her she'd

sucked her glass dry; but she'd wait a while before heading back in. Too many people who knew her name, who wanted to *know* her, made her feel smothered.

Funny, though Jim knew most of her story and wanted to know her more than any human on the planet did, it only made her crave more from him.

"Gets a bit overwhelming at times, all those people, when you don't know them, huh?"

The sun, low over the scrubby western hills, was shining right in her face. Squinting, she smiled up at Jim, standing over her like a big guardian angel. "I would feel it even if I did know them. I'm an only child, and my parents haven't got much extended family."

"It would take some getting used to," he agreed, his tone neutral. He handed her a cold, wet glass. "Drink more."

"Yes, dear," she mimicked with a grin, but she took the glass.

"I called Annie," he said quietly.

"Oh," was all she could think to say.

He shrugged. "I saved the number. I thought, while we're travelling—"

At his hesitation, she jumped into the breach. "Of course you want to meet her. When do we leave?"

Even in the gathering darkness, she could see his uncertainty. "You don't have to come with me, Danni. You've done enough."

Unable to take the squinting against the piercing final rays of sunlight, she shaded her eyes with one hand and patted the ground beside her. "I'm getting a crick in my neck looking up at you, Haskell. Come and talk to me."

"You don't have to come," he said as he slid down the tree to sit beside her. "I can drive you back first. The deal was coming with me here, to face my family."

It was as if he'd become devil's advocate for the feelings she'd admitted only moments ago. She shrugged. "Annie's your family, too," she pointed out.

His face darkened. He said nothing.

"Anyway, I've got a week, and for some unknown reason," she mocked herself, "my social calendar is empty. You're saving me from a week of moving boxes around."

"And from being forced to spend time with your parents," he suggested, his tone neutral.

She smiled wryly at him. Of course he wouldn't leave it unsaid. If he had family problems to face, so did she…and going with him to meet Annie was putting it off for another few days. "Thanks for the reminder." Both her parents had called again today, which was why she'd come out here in the first place. Going through the Inquisition on her relationship with Jim, with his family all around her, was too embarrassing to contemplate.

"We can go from Annie's to see your parents, if you like. I owe you big-time for everything you've done for me, and," he added, laughing, "they think I'm a handsome dude, and one of the good guys. I might need the admiration society by then."

The thought that she might need him to face her parents raised her hackles, but it was brief—as was the fear she'd felt only minutes before. In the ten years she'd known Jim, she'd never seen anyone able to fight around him. He'd stop them sniping at each other in front of him—he had a way of soothing people, just by his presence, or with a few words.

Except with me, she thought, with a sense of fatality. He could soothe her fears and worries with a smile, a laugh, but even sitting here in deep conversation about their parental turbulence, every part of her still tingled.

He'd been doing this to her for years. No

wonder she'd avoided him so much before, pretended to dislike him. She'd *hated* his power over her, and part of her hated it still; but knowing he wanted her the same way had tossed aside barriers she'd had in place most of her life, and for the life of her, she couldn't put them back up.

"Thanks—I'd like it if you came with me." She knew her smile was loaded with the feminine shyness she couldn't hold in.

His eyes grew darker as he took in her undeniable desire, and a voice inside her began singing. *He wants me.*

"It's beautiful out here," she said to string out the glorious feeling. "Every time I'm in the outback, it grabs me. It has a feel to it you just don't get anywhere else."

"Yeah." He looked around the open land surrounding the small acreage his parents owned, the land around it that was untameable. "It's living land. It speaks to you while you're near it, and calls you back when you're not."

"It makes you feel as if your problems are small." She took a deep breath. "Even the air's different out here, and the sun too. Bigger, cleaner—"

"Hotter," he laughed. "Redder."

She pushed him with a shoulder. "So when do we head Annie's way?"

"Tomorrow suit you?" His voice was quiet again, too quiet, and she wished she'd kept up the banter. "I love everyone, but—"

She nodded. She knew. Fifty or so people wanting you to be healed, to be what you had been, when half of you was still missing—the expectation was too much, too soon. The love, the *hope* that he would go back to the man he'd been a week ago was a burden he couldn't take on his shoulders right now. "Tomorrow's fine."

"You held your own this morning with my parents," he said abruptly.

Uncomfortable with talking about it—her feelings on the subject of what she'd said, and why she'd said it, were too raw—she took another gulp of her drink. "So did you."

He didn't allow her distraction. "It can't have been easy to say something like that, just so you could stay with me." His voice was filled with hidden darkness. She glanced at him; his eyes were deep midnight. Holding so much inside he wasn't sharing with her—or, she suspected, with anyone. "I want you to know how much I appreciate what you did for me."

Squelching the urge to squirm, she shrugged. "I told you I wouldn't leave you alone. It was the only thing I could think to say at the time."

"Sometimes being impulsive is the best thing to do."

She smiled, a little. "I wouldn't know. I'm not good friends with impulsiveness."

"No," he agreed without inflection. "You'd rather be safe."

Startled, she stared at him. It was as if he'd reached right into her head and plucked her most intimate thoughts. "Nothing wrong with being safe."

"Yet the past two days you've lived on instinct, and it's worked out pretty well—for you as well as me."

The warm, teasing tone made her insides go mushy…for though a house full of people was less than thirty feet away, it felt as if they were alone in the outback. Intimate, sensual…and she knew what he was thinking.

What *she* was thinking.

What he wanted.

What *she* wanted.

I'll wait until you come to me.

The next move was hers.

"Yes," she said, hearing the husky note, unable to stop it. "I have been—impulsive."

"And it's been pretty damn good." His gaze dropped to her mouth.

She closed her eyes. "Yes." The word grated like sandpaper on glass, rough-edged with dangerous desire.

"No, Danni," he whispered in her ear. "Look at me. Don't hide."

Slowly, she lifted her lids and stared into eyes of velvet darkness, male and needing. Her whole body began to quiver.

"I'm here. Your call. Your decision to come to me, or not," he murmured. His breath, warm and sweet like pineapples, washed over her skin.

And though he hadn't touched her, she shuddered with longing.

Sensuous power without force—Jim was too much a man to need to push his will onto her. He'd told her what he wanted. He'd made his move, one step closer to her on this intricate chessboard of desire.

Her heart was pounding so hard it left the rest of her body shaking and weak; her lungs refused to work properly. Her hands were trembling so much she had to put the glass down. As she moistened her mouth, she saw his gaze follow her tongue moving across her mouth, lazy and hungering at once.

There…there were reasons…this was a bad idea. Wasn't it? She couldn't remember, couldn't think…

Ah, it felt so *good* to wind her fingers through his hair, she thought hazily as her eyes fluttered shut and she drew him to her.

As his warm, full mouth covered hers, she heard a whimper and was amazed anew to discover she could make that needy sound. But oh, it was *lethal* what he could do to her.

Death by desire…yes, oh, *yes*…

Dimly she realised she was back on his lap, her arms in a stranglehold around his neck, and she was kissing him as if she were starving and he was ambrosia. Some dim part of her knew she ought to be terrified—this kind of mindless passion was what had led her mother to disaster—but she couldn't think long enough to care. She was where she needed, ached to be. Nothing had ever felt so right or utterly beautiful as being with this man. In a life of isolation and hard work and running from anything close to emotion, she'd found glorious haven, right in the eye of an emotional storm.

The beauty was worth the personal sacrifice of her privacy—it was worth *everything*. Finally she wasn't a dead woman hiding beneath warm skin; she was *alive*. A real woman at last, wanting a man…

Jim. Wanting only Jim.

"How the hell have we known each other so many years and not known *this* was here waiting for us?" he mumbled against her lips, kissing her over and over.

She couldn't answer, couldn't *speak* if her life depended on it, but the knowledge, the name came at once, shocking her from her sweet dream with a sword slash.

Laila, my best friend. Just as Mum's competition had been her friend…

Like cold water doused over her, she jumped away from him, panting.

"Damn it, Danni, don't look at me like I've betrayed you," he growled. "I didn't touch you. It was your choice."

It wasn't you that betrayed me, but my own body, my heart. Oh God help me, I'm turning into my mother, wanting a man who loves another woman, taking him anyway.

The thing she'd tried to fight all her life was

happening to her, and she couldn't stop it. She knew Jim wasn't in love with Laila anymore—but the fact remained, the history unchangeable. He'd ignored her for years, seeing only her friend.

It was her mother's history repeating.

She scrambled off his lap so fast she landed on her hands and knees on the ground, crying out in the sudden yank of pain.

"Are you all right?" Before she knew it, she was back on his lap and he was inspecting her wounds.

"I'm fine." Somehow she forced the words out of a frozen throat. "Look, the timing for this couldn't be worse. We—we should stay friends."

Softly he blew the tiny sharp rocks from her palms, one after the other, and the treacherous heat rushed through her again. "Yeah? You think friends often kiss the way we just did, the way we've constantly done the past day, and can just forget it?"

She felt the blush cover her face. "I don't know," she snapped, snatching her hands back, "but I don't want more."

He looked into her eyes and whispered, "Liar."

With the dark challenge in his eyes, she couldn't force the lies from her throat. "So I want you, Haskell—sue me. It's not going to happen, not while—while your life is in a state of flux." And that was the best she could do at a convincing excuse that wasn't a lie. "I think I'll see if your mother needs help with dinner."

"No." The low growl shocked her far more than the arms holding her still. "Stop running from me, Danni. You can't spend your life playing hide-and-seek with everyone who gets close to you, or every time your emotions or your passion frightens you. You have to take a risk sometime, reach out and trust that it won't always end up as it did for your family." He smiled again, his eyes dark and sleepy. "Sometimes there's even a happy ending, like my parents. Like Laila and Jake."

How did he *know* her deepest-held fear, and just bring it out into the open so damn *casually?* That he could read her so easily didn't just frighten her—it *terrified* her, and her helplessness morphed into hot anger. "You have no right to tell me what I can and can't do. Last night, you learned how fast the rug can be pulled from underneath you, right? Well, I never *had* any security to lose. Unlike you, I don't have half a town willing to toss out their day to see if I'm all right—all I have is parents who hate each other's guts and live only to get me on their side. So if I'm screwed up, I have good reason!"

She pushed at him to release her, and slowly, he did. His gaze searched hers, but he didn't speak. Waiting for the rest.

She moved off his lap and crouched in front of him. Panting, she went on, because she was too furious to stop. "I don't have a clue how you must feel right now, discovering you're adopted, but you know what? *I'd like to!* Part of me is sick with envy—not just because you're so damn *loved*, but because you can be *free* of all these people now if you want to be. Sometimes I'd give anything to *not* belong to the two most messed-up people I know! You think I'm scared? Tell me how it feels, then, because *I don't know*. I don't know anything about love or happiness. Apart from my work, I don't know anything but hate and bitterness—and you don't deserve to get lumped with an emotional train wreck like me!"

Darkness fell at that moment, like a thick curtain falling over them…and Danni was glad of it because she'd never made such a fool of herself before. *Why* had she done it? She wanted him like crazy, so why was she doing her best to push him out of her life? The things she'd just said were architect-designed to make any man bolt in the other direction.

Yet when his warm voice came to her, it was filled with something like tenderness; it touched her shivering soul with caring. "I think you've waited years to say that."

He was right; and like a candle snuffed, her fight left her. "Yes," she mumbled.

"To me. You've wanted to say it to me, haven't you?"

She almost choked on the word; but she couldn't hide, not now he'd accused her of cowardice, now he had seen and dissected the shivering child inside her. "Yes."

"Want to tell me why?"

"Because you have so *much* love in your life, yet you felt sorry for yourself because one woman didn't want you." Spent, she turned away before she blurted out the one truth she had to hide. *Because I wanted to be the woman you looked at as if she were the most beautiful thing on the planet. Because I resented you like hell for not seeing me!*

She knew that now, and she wouldn't hide from it—but telling Jim was impossible. She'd risked enough emotional suicide for one day, and it couldn't be worse timing. Jim had enough to cope with.

"You were jealous, weren't you, Danni?" he asked softly. "Jealous of her, your best friend, because you wanted to be the one with me."

She choked on the word; she *refused* to say it. She turned and fled into the house—but not before the words floated into her consciousness.

"Did you always want me, and I was blind to it?"

He should have known better than to say the words aloud; but when she'd tried to bolt back into her safe place of hiding inside herself, he'd wanted to push her into an emotional corner, to make her admit—

What? That she more than wants me? That she has feelings for me?

What the hell would I do with it, even if she'd said it?

The hell of it all was he didn't know. She was right; his life was in a state of flux and it would unravel only in its own time and way. He couldn't work out how he felt about his adopted parents, his real parents, and he resented the easy acceptance everyone in his family had about his life. It was okay for them to say accept it and move on—to say his parents had done the right thing for everyone concerned. Lies were lies, and he *hated* them.

At least he'd stopped Danni's lies. She wasn't sweet; she wasn't reasonable—she was a hot handful, spice instead of sugar, and he liked her that way. He didn't want her to become the imitation of Laila she'd tried to be in the car this morning. Much as he cared about her, he didn't want Laila here. Damned if he knew why, but Danni's blend of passion and acerbity was exactly what he needed.

There was no way he *could* know how he felt about anything right now, least of all Danni. So was it fair of him to push her?

All he knew was he wasn't going out with a whimper, the way he had with Laila. He hadn't fought her decision that her love was only as a friend, a sister—maybe he'd always known it was useless—but Danni wanted him even when she was tearing-strips-off-him mad. He only had to look at her, whisper a few words, and she melted for him. He could make her come to him with a crook of his finger.

So strong, yet so feminine. So independent, yet she couldn't deny her desire for him, his little fighter. He wanted her like crazy—he only hoped that in trying to force her closer, he hadn't driven her away for good.

She was still here. Even though it was obviously hurting her to do so, she kept to her word. She wouldn't leave him alone in his ordeal. She would stand beside him, be a conscious shield against his family's loving anxiety, and when he met Annie.

For the first time in his life, he had a woman who would stand by him when his life hit the emotional fan, and still wanted him.

Only now, she couldn't look him in the eye. Those shy, feminine smiles—the raw, innocent, coming-to-life sensuality she hadn't been able to hide—were replaced by the plastic smiles of a woman blindly playing a part of a lover to keep his family happy.

He wouldn't *let* it be over before it began! Whatever this was, it was too strong to walk away from. He'd done that once, it wasn't going to happen this time.

Dinner consisted mostly of meat. Danni picked the pasta out as discreetly as possible, leaving the sauce, pleading the heat of the day for her lack of appetite instead of embarrassing his mum by telling her she was vegetarian when it was too late to do anything about it.

She was a good person. Did she know that about herself? She didn't even seem to feel awkward about being the only full-blood Caucasian in the house. She chatted to everyone, played with the kids in the afternoon, swinging off the tyre into the river, playing cards.

Helping his mum with dinner, making meat sauce as though she did it every day.

She roped him into doing the dishes with her after dinner, and he decided to test the waters, allowing his hand to brush over hers, seemingly by accident. Smiling at her in the way he knew she couldn't resist. Maybe she'd say something impulsive again. Or she might *do* something, like sock him—or kiss him. He smiled, anticipating whatever she'd do, because *any* response meant she wasn't indifferent to him.

As she washed, using his mother's gloves, her hair kept falling in her face. She kept blowing it back, getting madder by the moment in her ineffectiveness.

He grinned as he brushed it back for her. "Better?" he asked softly.

"Stop it," she muttered, her face flushed, her

eyes sparking with anger. "I know what you're doing, and it isn't working."

He squelched the urge to laugh. He lifted his hands in mock-innocence. "Just trying to be helpful."

She jerked back, her eyes hunted. "You said you wouldn't touch me first."

He leaned into her. "My words were I wouldn't touch you until you came to me, Danni. And you did."

Her lower lip pushed out. Danni Morrison, tough-talking poster girl for scaring men off, was actually *pouting*, and it had to be the cutest thing he'd ever seen. "I take it back."

His grin grew. "What, are we in kindergarten now?"

He gasped and staggered back when he was doused in hot soapy dishwater.

"Yeah, you go, girl," one of his uncles cheered on good-naturedly from the dining table as Jim stared down at his soaked clothes. "Dunno what he did, but he deserves it."

"He always was a tease," his mum said, smiling at him.

"I told you to stop it," Danni all but shouted at him, so mad she ignored the laughing taunts and encouragement from his family. "I was awake all last night. I'm exhausted and I'm cranky. I just want to do the dishes and go to bed, and you're driving me *crazy*!"

"Hit him. Hit him!" one of his cousins yelled.

Everyone gathered around from the open-plan living area, laughing.

And though the turbulence of the day was with him still, Jim couldn't stop grinning. He tipped his hand into the dishwater and flicked a handful at her before she could jump away.

She gasped, looked down at her dripping top and jeans, and lifted her face to his.

So stunned that any man would fight back, that a man would make fun of her, tease her and yes, there was a tiny twinkle lurking in her eye…

"Go for it, tiger," he whispered, smiling for her alone.

Her mouth scrunched up; her eyes narrowed and she flicked water in his face.

He tossed some back, loving that she didn't bother with make-up. She was just as beautiful with water and soap bubbles dripping down her face…

And he was finding it hard to breathe.

Danni's chest heaved as if she'd run a race.

Though he vaguely realised his family had made themselves scarce, he couldn't take it in; he couldn't *see* anything but Danni. His gaze devoured her, and she couldn't take her eyes from him.

Did he snatch her up, or did she run to him? He didn't know. All he knew was they were kissing again, their wet bodies locked together, and even with her hands encased in soaking multipurpose gloves, he'd never felt so *much* in his life....

Wrong time, wrong place, wrong people. He knew all the arguments, but it didn't matter. This thing between them was unavoidable, uncontrollable. He and Danni were lives colliding from opposite ends of the universe, somehow making everything balance. Two wrongs making something very right.

Too fast, too sudden, he knew this was crazy—yet it all made *sense* with Danni in his arms, kissing him as if she'd been waiting for him all her life.

As if she'd heard his thought, she pulled back, looking at him with dark, sombre eyes. "This is going too fast."

Somehow he'd expected that. He nodded. "I know."

"There's too much happening. The timing couldn't be worse."

"I was just thinking that myself," he agreed. "But—"

She sighed. They both knew that, when they touched, timing and family messes just didn't matter. "Yes. *But*."

Wondering why she didn't move out of his arms, he asked, "Do you want me to take you back to Bathurst?"

"It would be…the sensible thing to do."

He jumped on the reluctance in her tone, but didn't push her. "I'll do it if you want me to—but I don't want you to go."

"I don't want to go," she whispered, her eyes huge. She twined one of his curls around her gloved finger. "I want to be with you."

His arms tightened around her. "I can't promise not to touch you."

Her head fell to his shoulder. "I think I'd kill you if you *didn't*."

He chuckled, holding her close, loving the feel of her against him, around him, with a possessive flash he'd never known with a woman before. "So we agree—we're *not* friends?"

She looked up again, with a wistful glance that

made him ache to kiss her. "Do you think we can be friends? I—I've always wanted to be your friend, but this *thing*—it was always there, this massive obstacle in the way...."

Oh, *man*... Joy streaked like lightning through every part of his body at the implications of her words. She liked him, she respected him, and she wanted him. The combination he'd looked for all his life from a woman who *mattered*. "Friends and lovers?" he asked huskily.

A slow smile curved her mouth. "Don't push me, Haskell. I've said all I'm going to for one day. I've been impulsive enough."

He grinned and kissed her, deep and slow. Revelling in the soft whimpers she made, the helpless response he could tell she loved, much as she still tried to fight it. "Then let's finish these dishes, and get some rest. I have to sort out the tent and sleeping gear." At her inquiring look—with remnants of the flushed, starry-eyed arousal in her eyes—he added, "Annie's at a sheep station over the South Australian border. It's right off the beaten track. It'll take us a couple of days to get there, and there's not many places to stay on the road."

She frowned and moved out of his arms, withdrawing from him emotionally as well as putting physical distance between them.

No doubt wondering what she'd gotten herself into with him again.

Sensible, straight-talking Danni was off balance between needing to run and wanting to stay with him—and that was mammoth progress in twenty-four hours.

It was more than he'd expected, yet it wasn't enough. He wanted more, so much more. He needed her in a way he'd never needed a woman before. He'd spent his life being the giver, yet discovering the sweetness of Danni's sensual awakening had made this poignant homecoming somehow bearable. She'd made it all right— he'd been in control, instead of being here to listen, to fix everyone's problems.

But that was what happened in families. Everyone had their role. He was the repairer. It was what he did—and he had the education and money to help out. He'd done so for as long as he could remember, but though they all liked beer, and a couple of his uncles were questionable, nobody in his immediate family was a drunk or drug addict. He hadn't rescued anyone in *that* way.

So he liked to help people! It didn't make him an *enabler.* Maybe she'd been half-right—he did fix things for everyone—but he hadn't made anyone in his family weak or reliant on him. If they were, he'd be living here, not in Cooinda. And if he was always here for them, they were always there for him, too.

Adopted or not, he couldn't deny the bond of love was real and strong. He belonged here; this was his place.

And needing Danni wasn't as scary as he'd thought it would be when he knew she'd never felt so much wanting for a man before him.

So be sure it's what you want, a little voice inside warned him. *Don't hurt her.*

And that was the voice of reason. If Danni made one hell of a good friend—and a lover beyond anything he'd known—he'd never forgive himself if she got caught in the crossfire of the lie his life had become.

But though he had no idea how or why, Danni had become vital to him in the past twenty-four hours. Her support made him less alone; her very presence calmed the turmoil inside him; her smile took away the pain, and her touch made him forget everything but her.

And the spice of her fight against wanting him as much as she did made the challenge sweeter, when he knew she couldn't resist him.

He didn't care how bad the timing was. He *needed* Danni, even more than he wanted her. He didn't know what the hell was going on, for it sure wasn't the deep, quiet certainty of love he'd had with Laila—but what he felt for Danni was too intense to walk away from.

CHAPTER SIX

I am reading this.

ALMOST THE ENTIRE HASKELL CLAN came the next morning to wave them off.

Danni felt sadness bloom in her chest and across her soul at the small sea of smiling faces. They were all there for Jim, willing to accept her, a stranger into the family, because Jim liked her. His parents hadn't even thought of punishing her for her initial rudeness, or Jim's insistence that she be included in their family business.

They might have wanted more acceptance from Jim than he'd been able to give at the time, but at least they knew how to give back to him…and they did.

She turned to look at him once the faces had finally faded into a wider vista of hot earth tones all around them. "You okay?"

He smiled at her. "I will be."

"I don't doubt it." She couldn't help the touch of dryness in her tone.

He cocked a brow. "What's up, Danni-girl?"

She shrugged, wondering again why she didn't and had never bristled against the nickname; she'd always hated them before. "Just thinking about the differences between us." Turning her face, she looked out the tinted window to the dramatic landscape outside. She'd never been this far north in her work experience, and the stark magnificence of untamed earth took her breath—and a measure of calm seeped into her chaotic soul. "If this had happened to me, I'd be a mess for months, maybe years to come. But after the initial shock, you just seem to be taking it in your stride. You adjust so easily."

"Maybe I'm just better at hiding it than you."

His tone had lost the lightness. Turning back, she saw nothing on his face: it was completely calm. "If you say so." There was no way she'd ever be able to hide her feelings—

But then, she wasn't the oldest of six children, all close in age. He'd probably learned to put his emotions and needs on the backburner by the time he was two.

"I doubt birthdays are ever going to be the

same now," he joked, but it sounded flat. "And I could have been taken away if Mum and Dad hadn't lied on my birth certificate." He shrugged again. "There's years of psychoanalysis in just those two issues."

Danni sighed. He didn't know it, but he'd shut the door by the way he'd said it, as if it didn't matter—and she knew he'd never take the help if it was right in front of him. "Did your—did Annie tell you why she called?" She'd been bursting with curiosity on this point, but had determined to wait and see if he'd tell her.

Obviously that wasn't going to happen. In fact, for a man whose life had turned upside down in an hour, he'd said very little to her about his feelings about his adoption.

"She said she was sick." Again, he sounded calm—too calm. He looked straight ahead at the road.

His knuckles showed beneath his skin, he was gripping the wheel so hard.

A wave of fellow feeling washed through her. She knew so well how it felt to hurt, to wonder what the *hell* was up with parents, hiding stuff and lying when it was so pitifully obvious they were lying. "You didn't believe her?"

His mouth hardened. "I don't know her. What reason do I have to disbelieve her?"

Gently, she said, "It's a common instinct for natural mothers to find their children."

"Maybe." He shrugged. "There's a lot of potholes on the road, and a ton of wombats out here. Got to take care."

He was shutting the door on her; and though she knew she should back off, her hackles rose. "How do you feel about your adopted parents, and that they never told you the truth when others obviously knew? Didn't it hurt to see them all there, realising they'd known all along, and you didn't?"

He pressed the CD player button, and started singing as if he hadn't heard.

From her psychology classes she knew she should expect this silence, and respect it—but the woman in her rose up in hot rebellion. "Why am I here? Why am I bothering if all you're going to do is shut me out?"

After a short silence, he said with a tight jaw, "You offered."

"Why didn't you say thanks but no thanks, if all I was going to be was spare luggage or for you to lay bare my life and faults?"

"Maybe you needed both those experiences,"

he snapped. "It was time you learned people aren't as scared off by your sarcastic quips as you think."

"Big, brave Jimmy," she mocked—at least he was speaking now about something other than the road and wildlife.

He shrugged again. "Someone had to tackle your fear of intimacy sometime."

Without warning, she became *really* mad. "My fear of intimacy. *Mine?*" She laughed in his face. "Yeah, my terror of closeness is so obvious right now, isn't it? Wake up and smell the denial, Haskell! I've been spilling my guts to you for thirty-six hours straight, while you haven't said a single word to me or anyone else about your feelings. You're projecting your own behaviour onto me!"

"Are we up to your second-year psychology training yet?" he sneered.

She flipped her hands up. "This is classic enabler behaviour again. You can give and give, and push everyone else out of their caves, but God help the person who tackles your fears and deepest feelings. That's why you fell for Laila," she taunted, to make him mad enough to really *say* something. "She *needed* you, big, strong

Jimmy, to make her life right. She thought you were so wonderful, didn't she? She took you right back to your comfort zone, looking after her just as you look after everyone else. But who was there for *you*, Jim?" she added in sudden sadness, when it was obvious he was retreating back into silence. "Who stood by you when your life fell apart?"

He turned his face and stared at her, shock written in every feature. Without conscious thought he pulled the car over to the side of the dirt road, though it wouldn't have mattered if he'd stopped in the middle of a road where maybe fifteen cars passed in an entire day.

It's now or never, Danni-girl, she thought, hearing the echo of his nickname for her in a kind of weary acceptance. She didn't *want* this to mean more to her than any moment in her life before, but it did…because *Jim* meant more to her than she wanted him to. He'd gotten beneath her skin by surprise attack, and all her usual weapons had proven useless. How did she stop him, when he didn't battle by her rules?

Trying to fight *his* way, she touched his cheek, and felt his flinch, his retreat—but she couldn't stop now. "It's a sad testament to all your giving, that only *I* came out to you that night, and we weren't even friends. All those people you'd spent years giving to couldn't be bothered getting their butts off their chairs for you. They weren't about to leave their comfort zones for you, because *you're* the giver, the listener, the helper. They take, all those people—even Laila did."

"Leave Laila out of this," he snarled, turning the engine off with a savage click.

Danni shook her head, feeling driven to say it, driven to make him *see*. She didn't look at why; she hid from her emotions like a child under a blanket in the darkness. "You know how much I love her, Jim, but when things were falling apart with Jake, who did she call? The other man in love with her! How cruel was it of her to do that? I know she didn't *mean* to hurt you, but she needed you, and she knew you'd come. You can't resist a cry for help…and she knew you'd sacrifice your own feelings to help her."

"I don't want to talk about it." Fury filled every syllable.

"Too bad, because you *have* to see it if you're ever going to come to terms with the past couple of days," she said, risking it all on one throw. Her knowledge of his innate kindness told her he wouldn't toss her out of the car. "Tell me something, Jim—do you think Laila would sacrifice her emotions to help you? The other night she wouldn't come out to you. She said it was Braxton-Hicks contractions, but the truth was, it was because of Jake. She didn't want him to feel insecure—she wouldn't risk upsetting him even when her best friend, who'd always come to help her, was in such obvious pain."

After another long, uncomfortable silence, he sighed. "Go on, *Dr. Morrison*. I'm sure you have the full diagnosis you're dying to drop on my lap."

She stared down at her own lap as she let the words out that yes, she was dying to say. Knew she had to be cruel—to make him feel. "Like everyone else that night, Laila didn't come out to you because *you're* the giver. And though I know she calls you and asks about your life, I'd be willing to bet that within thirty seconds, you turn it all back to Laila. Because you're the listener—*you* want it that way. Giving allows you your space and privacy. You don't have to drop down to the level of the rest of humanity, with all its fears and pain. But as you learned the other night, when you are in desperate need, Jim, who's there for *you*?"

A long stretch of quiet passed before she dared look up at him, and to her shock, he was smiling at her. "You were."

Her return smile was wry. "Only because Laila pushed me out the door," she admitted, breathless just from the curve of his mouth.

"Did she push you to come here with me, Danni?"

Feeling oddly shy, she dipped her head down. She knew she didn't have to answer.

"You said you always wanted to be my friend," he said quietly.

"That's why I'm here. Why I'm saying all this." Her voice cracked. "You give to everyone. I don't want you to save me or be my best friend—I want to be *your* friend. I want to give to you—and I want you to accept that you need it." She gulped when she'd finished taking the biggest risk of her life because this wasn't sensual, this was emotional risk. And the rejection would hurt far more than turning her down sexually. "Let me in, Jim. Tell me—"

"Danni."

At the warm, blurry voice, like a summer river, she looked up again. That wonderful face was hooded with shadows. "I can't tell you anything yet."

Her heart fell clear down to her toes, and oh, it hurt so much…she turned away so that he wouldn't see the tears gathering in her eyes. "Okay."

Strong arms encircled her, pulling her close, even as she resisted him, because physical closeness wasn't all she needed from him. She wanted more, so *much* more from him, heart and soul. "Danni-girl, ah, don't cry," he whispered into her hair. "I can't tell you what I don't know. I'm upside down and inside out. It's only been two days since my life blew apart. I need to meet her, to think about why my parents lied to me. I need time to reconstruct my life, to build again. Then I might know something besides the fact that I'm bloody angry. Leave me until I've met her. I don't want to take my anger out on you again. Okay?"

Hiding her face in his shoulder, she nodded. "I'm not crying," she said gruffly. "I never cry." But she didn't look up because she was petrified he'd see the turbulence in her eyes, the terror that she'd just made a discovery she'd never wanted in her lifetime.

The knowledge she'd already run from for almost a decade.

Love, her heart whispered. *You love him. You always have.*

Rubbish, her mind hissed right back. *What do you know about love? Nothing. And right now his life's a mess. Don't make him rely on you. You'll only confuse his feelings.*

He wanted her now, but that wasn't enough. *She* was inadequate, essential parts of her missing. She knew that from bitter experience. Reality was the best teacher. The woman she was could never be enough for a man like Jim.

Keeping it honest—just desire, pure and simple—was the only way they'd both survive the explosion their lives had become. Or at least, *his* life… Hers had always been this way.

As if he'd heard her heart's decision, he cuddled her closer. "Don't give up on me yet, Danni," he murmured. "Give me a chance…"

A shiver of longing ran through her, helpless, as unstoppable as it was impossible. "It's okay," she whispered because she didn't know what else to say. "We should go. I want to make it to a pub before dark."

"Don't you trust my camping skills?" His voice was rich with laughter now.

Wanting to leave behind the admission she might never be ready to make, she murmured, "Um…I didn't tell you this, but I've only camped once, on a school excursion, and—and a *thing* got in my tent, and crawled into my hair."

"I get it." He laughed out loud this time. "Scared the living daylights out of the entire local area?"

"Screamed like a banshee," she admitted with a little chuckle. "I pulled down the whole four-person tent trying to get it off me."

"How many years did it take you to get over that humiliation?"

She lifted her face to his then. "Why do you think I went to a university three hundred kilometres from Sydney, and never went camping again?"

He lifted a brow. "One day we have to talk about your unorthodox coping skills."

"When your own are back in place, you mean?" she taunted lightly.

"How well the woman knows me." But he was still grinning. His eyes lingered on her for another moment, warm and almost tender. Her heart skipped a beat, then he shook his head, released her and turned to start the car again.

* * *

Yeah, Jim admitted to himself as he broke the four-hour driving barrier and kept going, allowing Danni to sleep—and she really was asleep this time, worn out with all the travel and so little rest. *So I'm a giver, and more than a bit of a control freak.*

But it wasn't just that he didn't like anyone else driving his car—a leftover from the days of his old mighty Valiant, when one wrong move could almost make the engine drop out—he needed time to think, and doing something constructive always helped.

He knew he should be thinking of the upcoming meeting with Annie—with his natural mother. He should be answering one of the four calls his parents—his *adopted* parents—had made in the past hour. Of course they were anxious. They needed reassurance.

He had none to give them. Not until he met Annie, talked to her—and he didn't have a clue what he was going to say to her.

But truthfully, he wasn't even thinking of any of that. He couldn't stop thinking of the massive amount of risks Danni had taken in the past two days.

For him.

There was no other reason, could be none, apart from that she really did care. Prickly, abrasive, run-a-million-miles-from-emotion Danni was reaching out, being someone she wasn't in spilling her guts, as she'd put it—giving from her shielded heart, over and over.

Giving to him, for him alone. *For him.*

Since he'd never seen her let anyone in but Laila, this was a massive leap of faith for her. She trusted him.

Could there possibly be a worse time for a man to discover he was in love for the last time in his life?

No…it might be the last time, but he was also in love for the first *real* time in his life. Danni had been right—Maddy and Laila had both been needy types, who'd made him feel strong. And their relationships, both of them, had been based on his giving and their taking.

No wonder Maddy and Laila had both gone for other guys. No woman wanted to remain a victim forever. A woman liked an equal footing in a relationship, to be a strong and necessary part of it—he'd just never realised he'd never offered them that.

Until Danni had smashed down his imaginary

tower of strength and showed him for the man he was inside…and she wanted him anyway. She'd *never* accept less than equal footing, and he wouldn't dream of giving her less. Danni was no victim; she was a survivor, like him, and deserved the respect she demanded.

If he'd ever rescued Danni, she'd rescued him right back—and it wasn't as scary as he'd thought it would be. He wasn't any less a man for having someone to lean on.

But telling her was impossible. It was too new, too raw. It had only been two days since they'd seen each other again, and he had too much on his mind. He had to meet Annie first, to know why she'd left him with—with *Bob-and-Claire, Dad-and-Mum*—and told him who his father was.

Danni said he deserved more than an emotional train wreck. Well, so did she—and he had to make sure he could give it to her before he said anything. When he knew about his past, his family—when he knew *himself*—he might be able to put his life back together and make something of it.

With Danni, if she was willing. If he could be sure this was love. She'd been hurt enough for a lifetime.

He smiled to himself, imagining the battle

royal he had before him, just to convince her he was here to stay. Danni was no pushover; his words of love were more likely to make her punch him out than melt into his arms. She might want him like crazy, but committing herself to more than this week with him was a whole other animal. She'd spent too many years locked inside a cell with only the dark side of love and commitment to accompany her. She needed to not just *hear* about the sunlight and starlight, but to *see* it for herself. She needed to reach out with her own fingers and feel the miracle of life…and love.

He had to make her come to him, to tell him how she felt first. *If* she really did feel anything for him. If he could make her do more than just want him…

She stretched, yawned and frowned at that moment, looking at the state of the sky. "It's late afternoon," she mumbled, still half-asleep. "You were supposed to wake me for my driving shift."

He grinned at her. Every other woman he knew would have thanked him for his consideration; she'd made her words an accusation. "Yeah, but your snoring was so cute I couldn't do it."

To his secret delight, she blushed. "I snore?"

"Gotcha," he laughed and received the expected punch. "Ow."

"Where are we?"

"About two hours west of Nyngan."

She gasped. "You've been driving too long."

"I'm fine, Danni."

She shook her head, her face taking on the stubborn look he knew well. "Pull over and swap, Haskell. No arguing."

With a shrug, he pulled over on the dirt and gravel that passed for the side of the road.

"So where's the road map? Where's our destination tonight?" she asked as she took off.

"I don't want to go too much further today. She's shearing northwest of the Mallee—over into South Australia. We'll have another night on the road anyway. If the town's pub is full, we'll have to camp—and we don't want to set up tent by night," he added, teasing her.

She rolled her eyes. "I hope you cook, if we can't get into the pub. I'm good with Asian and Indian and salads, but the intricacy of outdoor cooking's beyond me."

"And you're an Aussie?" When she hit his arm again, he laughed. "I think we should get into the pub, or better yet, there might be a hamburger or pie shop."

"Outback veggie pies?" she asked with a wealth of wry humour in her tone. "Outback veggie burgers? Looks like I'll be eating chips with sauce."

He shrugged and laughed. "Okay, the pub it is—but it might not be safe for you."

She frowned at him for a moment, before she gave a wry grin. "What's the male-to-female ratio out here?"

"About eight men to one woman, I think—twenty to one if we're talking women of child-bearing age." He winked at her. "Your popularity will never be higher than at that pub tonight… and they like 'em tough out here."

He hadn't realised the test he'd set for her until her eyes deepened with thoughtfulness, she made a rueful face and said, "I wouldn't raise the hopes of some lonely man just to lift my ego, or let the town think they could get a vet out here when I'm not here to stay."

"You're a good woman, Danni Morrison," he said softly.

She lifted one side of her mouth, a tight, self-mocking grin. "I like to play fair."

His mind went over all the things she'd said since that night in Bathurst, and realised it was only half-true. Danni didn't play at all: she told blunt truth, and let him deal with the consequences of it. "I've noticed."

"My father didn't play fair that night with Mum—and Mum doesn't play fair now. And they've both suffered the past thirty years for it."

Jim almost flinched, thinking about what she really meant. It took him almost a full minute to say it, but in the silence, he knew she already knew what he would say, so he kept it simple. "And you?"

She nodded once. "And me." Looking straight ahead, she was as delicate, as remote as fairy motes dancing in the sunset dust, and just as tangible.

She'd gone far away from him. Her two words painted two thousand pictures.

A child of war who knew how to cope with the weapons of destruction, she went into voluntary withdrawal when the shells began hitting, hiding inside herself like a soldier in a bunker. If she chose to reach out and help others, she could do it—but it was on her terms. Passion she could explore—she'd proven that. But to *trust*, when she'd never once seen the happiness it could bring? To trust in love lasting, when she'd never seen or known it?

Drawn as much by her sadness as her addictive prettiness, he kept his gaze on her—but it hurt. Her face was alabaster-pale in the gathering dusk, reflecting the colours of sunset without taking them on. A cold mirror of ancient pain, there was light and life on the other side...but she kept it there. She was watching life pass her by. Part of her might hunger to become a true part of it, but she was too afraid to reach out and grab at the chance when it was right in front of her.

And that said it all.

No, he couldn't tell her how he felt. He had to make her need him first, to trust him enough to admit she could love him.

She had to leave her hiding places of emotional distance and come to him.

But how he was going to break the habits of a lifetime when she had so damn much still to hide from, in her parents' ongoing and not so very *civil* war, he didn't know.

CHAPTER SEVEN

IT WAS ONE THING TO KNOW YOU have to wait, another to do it.

Especially when you knew how much joy and passion sat only inches from your craving body…

Jim's life was in chaos. He didn't know who he was. There couldn't be a worse time to begin a relationship—if a relationship was what he wanted with her.

Danni knew it was the right and good thing to be patient until he'd met his mother, knew about his father, and came to terms with everything that had happened to him. But her body didn't know good sense. Rebellion was an explosion inside her, whispering, nagging and finally screaming. *Do it.*

It wasn't going to happen. It *so* wasn't going to happen. He was emotionally vulnerable right now. He needed her restraint, for her to be a friend—and she wouldn't know how to handle the inevitable heartbreak. She didn't have the survival skills inbred in Jim.

Take a chance, Danni-girl, her heart whispered, joining in the rebellion. *For once give yourself heart and soul to a man and see where it takes you both.*

She couldn't.

But after a life of good sense and abstinence—of *running* from emotion—her body had come to life and was locked in a constant battle against her will, all the way to the wire.

Though she didn't want to, she sneaked another peek at him, as she'd done every fifteen seconds since she'd taken driving shift.

He looked so peaceful. She couldn't do it to him. She *shouldn't* do it. He had another ordeal to face, meeting his mother, finding out why she'd abandoned him.

What would he do if she just stopped the car and threw herself at him?

You know what he'd do....

Suddenly the strains of a love song filled the quiet car, making her start. Jim sighed, coming out of sleep, and answered his phone sleepily. "Hey, babe?"

Danni's stomach tightened. She ought to have known who would have such a ring tone. No doubt if mobile phones had been invented thirty years ago, Dad's phone would have had a similar tone for the woman he couldn't stop loving.

Don't be stupid, he said he was over her. He probably just didn't bother changing the ring tone.

Yeah, he said it was over, but the ring tone sings another song, doesn't it?

Trying to conquer the demon of jealousy in her mind even she knew was unreasonable, she kept driving, looking straight ahead. Wishing it didn't have to be her best friend in the world who made her heart fill with this darkness. She didn't *want* to resent Laila…or be jealous but neither did she want to be the woman who was second best for Jim, the woman he'd take because the love of his life had married another man.

And this was why *predictable* was good. These three days had been unpredictable, and she was becoming everything she most hated, jealous and angry, her heart was breaking and she was even going to lose Laila, her best friend, because of it.

This was why she lived alone. She'd reached out, taken chances—and look where she was now. Lost in a seething mass of jealousy and anger that felt all too familiar—because she'd seen it on another woman's face, heard it in her voice for too many years.

"Nah, it's all cool. I'll tell you about it someday. Not now." Danni felt his glance touch her. "Yeah, Danni's still here with me."

At Danni's frantic head shake, he frowned and said, "But she's driving. She'll call you back later, okay?"

Jim and Laila talked a little more, Jim turning the subject to Ally and the upcoming baby with flawless skill. Jim the giver, doing what he did best.

When he flipped the phone shut, he said, "Danni? What is it?"

If she spoke now, she'd only say something he'd hate and she'd regret.

Danni shook her head, offered him a smile even *she* knew was brittle, and turned on the CD player. She couldn't talk to him until she found some semblance of calm inside herself—until she wrested the sickening, destructive jealousy out of her system. That feeling of being second best.

In another ten years, maybe.

* * *

The next night they crossed the South Australian border by sundown.

They'd made the crossing just below Cameron's Corner, the sign that marked the border between New South Wales, Queensland and South Australia. This was real, raw outback, where the hand of man lost against the toughest Nature could throw. You'd see a pub-cum-post-office-petrol-station and general store, and a garage-tyre sales outpost attached, every hundred kilometres if you were lucky. Farther into the state, on the Stuart Highway, there were more pubs and caravan parks, but that was hundreds of kilometres past where Annie was shearing. Out here, it was called *the back of beyond* because there was almost nothing here but vast, red, scrubby emptiness.

Danni had never been so far west in her life before, and the call of the outback was even stronger here—a song reverberating in her spirit she'd never known. Vast beyond imagining, allowing intrusion yet resisting invasion—nature did not rule here; it just *was*. Unchangeable, unmoving, harsh and unforgiving, yet it was part of her: an entity without human rules.

She knew something in her had changed even before she'd agreed to come here with Jim…that she was finally ready to reach out to life. Now life had touched her back, grabbing her by her very soul. She would never be the same.

Then another thought, tiny, ridiculous yet persistent, and so damn *human,* intruded on her journey and wouldn't let go. Or was it part of the journey, forcing her growth? She didn't want to know, but had no choice.

Tonight they had to camp….

"Jim. *Jim!*"

He'd scrambled out of his sleeping bag and grabbed his torch, heading for the tent before he thought to ask what the problem was. Danni's scream would wake the dead.

He didn't think about the tense, near-silent twenty-four hours since Laila's call last night, demanding "details" of what had happened that night at the restaurant, and was going on between him and Danni now. He didn't remember her conscious withdrawal, putting more distance between them than he could have imagined after their kisses, and all the time she'd spent trying to help him through his ordeal. All he knew was Danni needed him now. "Danni, what is it?"

He tore into the tent as she screamed again. She was hopping from foot to foot, her face pale and terrified. The moment he entered, she flung herself at him. "Th-there's something in my sl-sleeping bag. It *crawled* on me...."

He held back a blink of shock—a *vet* was scared of small creatures? But that kind of oxymoron epitomised the living conflict that was Danni. He squelched an urge to chuckle, not *at* her, but in sheer happiness that she trusted him enough to allow him to see her so vulnerable. He dropped to his knees—his head was pushing the tent off its pegs—and held her close. "It's okay, Danni-girl. Give me a minute. I'll find it and get it out."

"No. *No!*" She shuddered against him, clinging like a child. "Stay with me."

Even knowing she'd punish him later for showing her weakness, he let her bury her face in his shoulder. "No hardship," he murmured huskily, loving the feel of her all soft and warm and needing him.

"I'm *sorry.* So stupid," she whispered, her arms almost strangling him. "Can't—stand—creepy-crawlies, especially in the darkness…"

This wasn't the moment to ask why. If she wanted him to know, she'd tell him. "It's okay, baby. Nothing to be ashamed about. We all have our fears. If we have to set up camp again, I'll rig up a night-light, and get some bug repellents."

"I hate being so weak." Cranky about her dependence, yet wearily accepting it. She always had to fight something, his Danni.

"I know," he murmured huskily, trying *not* to think of how *wonderful* it felt to have her against and around him like this. "Don't be afraid to tell me your fears. I won't tease you."

"I'm afraid of *you*," she whispered, shaking still.

His heart melted at her vulnerability, and gave back to her. "You scare the hell out of me, too, Danni-girl. You make me think and feel too many things I don't want to know about. I liked my cave," he admitted, hoping he'd got it right. That it would make her feel better.

She pulled back with a tentative smile. "I guess we're two of a kind." Her eyes twinkled just a bit. She knew, just as he did, that the cave might keep her out of the way of pain, but living alone in cold, safe darkness wasn't enough, would never be enough. Not now.

Two of a kind. Belonging together?

"Ah, Danni," he murmured, brushing back her hair. Aching to kiss her, to connect—

"The—*thing…*"

He chuckled then. She wouldn't kiss him once he'd rid her sanctum of whatever had invaded it and she was back in control, but he didn't care. Again, he'd made progress, if she'd trusted him with one of her fears. Gently he put her down and handed her the torch. "Shine it for me."

The light remained steady as he dug his hands deep into the sleeping bag. She was reasserting control, and he was glad of it. Now he knew the joy of being with a woman who wanted him beyond what help he could give, he never wanted to go back. When she came to him, it would be as an equal: a woman in love with her man, wanting to be partners for life.

He would accept no less from her, and he'd make damn sure she would give no less.

A squeak and the feel of teeth digging into his hand told him he'd hit paydirt. He swore, but kept his hand wrapped around the tiny, wriggling creature, pulling it from the bag. "I think it's a wild mouse."

"Is it all right?" she cried. It seemed her fear

was only of bugs—a good thing since she was a vet. "Poor little thing must be terrified. Did I hurt it?"

He grimaced. "Not sure yet, but it's hurting me all right." He pulled it right out and plopped it into her open hand. "Check it out. I'll dig out my bag. I might need a shot."

"You haven't had your shots recently?" Her voice was low, soothing, as she turned the mouse over, checking for damage with expert fingers. "She seems fine. I'll put her out."

"I've had my tetanus teeters. I might need anti-biotics, though." He opened the tent flap for her to pass through.

"I'll do it. Just let me release the mouse—and zip the tent back up."

If he hadn't promised not to tease her, he'd have laughed. Instead, he zipped downward with a solemn air. "All done."

She turned her face to smile at him…and he caught his breath with the combination of delicate face, big eyes and clear moonlight. That she was wearing bright green PJs with the words Boys Have Cooties all over them only charmed him more. "Thank you."

She crossed the campsite to some scrubby

grass and rocks to release the mouse, while he opened the car and took out his treatment kit.

She was beside him moments later. "Let me see the wound."

He showed her his hand. "It's no big deal."

"She broke the skin, Jim. You need a shot."

He grinned. "I know that. I'm the country vet, Danni."

She broke the glass ampoule, drew up the broad-spectrum antibiotic and injected him at the deltoid. "Where's your first aid?"

At her insistence, he let her clean and disinfect the wound.

"I know it's ridiculous, a vet who has a fear of bugs," she said as she worked. Her hands were shaking, just as her voice was. "But I am getting better. It used to be any animal except for dogs, cats or birds. I used to be terrified of horses."

"That's why you wanted to become a vet, wasn't it?" But he knew the answer; he just wanted to peel away another layer of her defences. The more he came to know her, the more she wanted him. And she didn't know how much she needed to give her fears and worries to someone who cared about her. "Fighting the fear, wanting to beat it."

She sighed and nodded. "Mostly." She frowned in concentration as she painted the bite with Betadine. "So now you know why I don't like to camp. It always ends in disaster," she said as she bound his hand with a totally unnecessary bandage.

"And the problem with that is…?"

She frowned at him. "Well…"

"Does life always have to be predictable, successful, to enjoy it?"

Her head tilted as she stared at him. Trying to work him out, he could tell. "Don't you think it's better that way? Surely you can't have enjoyed my screaming you awake at, um—" she checked her watch by the light of the moon "—2:40 a.m., or have a mouse biting you?"

Slowly, he shrugged. "Whatever gets me close to you works for me," he said, to see what she'd say.

Slam. The shutters came down so fast he almost felt the wind rushing in their wake. She clipped the bandage in place and moved back. "It's late. You need rest before you see Annie tomorrow."

The reference was deliberate. She wanted him to close down, as he had every time she'd mentioned Annie's name—

She was using his self-sufficient nature—*insular*, she called it—against him, to restore her own emotional distance.

Clever girl. Now, if only he knew why she'd suddenly gone from trying to get closer to him to running at the slightest thing…

When he heard the sound of the tent zipper ripping up, then down, he realised he'd fallen into another trap. While he'd been puzzling it out, she'd disappeared into the tent.

Grimly he shook out his sleeping bag, in case a scorpion or something else had crawled in while he'd been rescuing Danni. He climbed back into his makeshift bed out in the open, and stared up at the stars, wondering why the radar he'd had with her had disappeared without warning, leaving him in the dark with everything she was thinking and feeling.

She'd taken him body and soul in three days—or maybe it was in ten years. Hell, even he no longer knew how long this slow train of love had been coming at him. But now she was in retreat and he had no idea why. With his life in turmoil between one set of parents' lies and another's desertion, he had no weapons left to fight the battle going on inside Danni's mind.

CHAPTER EIGHT

THE ROAD SHIMMERED AHEAD of them as they drove down the final stretch toward the turnoff to Brinya Station. The heat was so pervasive it was warm in the car, even over the air-conditioning.

It wasn't the only thing shimmering and enveloping. Jim's silence carried with it an entire cargo of unspoken fear, doubt, hope and suffering—and Danni could do nothing about it. She'd distanced herself from him at the worst possible time, but he'd accepted it with a weary kind of politeness that hurt her far more than any of her parents' needle-sharp wit and biting sarcasm.

Jim wasn't the kind of man to give up even on hopeless causes. She was the one who always ran away, pretending it was just a life change she had to have.

Moving on was her mantra—her excuse for keeping her distance, or creating distance. If no one got too close, then she didn't *feel* anything. The ups and downs of life didn't affect her, and she didn't become bitter. Everything was placid, predictable.

Does life have to be predictable to enjoy it?

It was something she'd never questioned…yet looking at the careful neutrality in his face, covering a volatile cocktail of emotions he might have shared with her before she closed the door on him, she wondered if he was right. She might be safer this way, but she wasn't enjoying life as she had when she was in his arms, taking a risk.

"We're almost there, aren't we?" she said, when the silence hurt her ears with all its unspoken accusations of cowardice.

"About another two or three kilometres to the turnoff," he agreed, his voice neutral. He kept his gaze and concentration on the road.

"Does she know we're arriving?"

He nodded. "I called this morning. She's taking a couple of hours off. She can't get more. It's early shearing time."

The words didn't even hold irony. He expected no more from his own mother. He was no more to her than a break in shearing time.

She gulped, but the ball of pain in her throat

wouldn't move. Her parents might never win an award for their rearing skills, but she'd never had cause to doubt they both loved her. Her mother would toss aside any consideration to come to her, at any time.

Almost scared to reach out again, she asked, "How—how do you feel, Jim? What are you going to say to her?"

He didn't even glance at her. "She sounded as if she had something on her mind, so I'll probably just listen. Take my cues from her."

Aching to reach out to him, to let him know he wasn't alone, she touched his hand on the wheel. "Do you want me to come with you to meet her?"

"She doesn't mean anything to me beyond a source of information, Danni. I'll be fine. But thank you."

Gone was the warmth and teasing. The man she'd found irresistible had vanished, and while she wanted to understand that he needed to be this stranger to cope with all life had thrown at him, she ached and burned with the craving to help, to touch him.

It was too late now. She'd walked away, and he'd let her go.

She didn't speak again, even when he turned in at the Brinya Station sign.

So here they were.

He sat in the car staring at the gate, a silent Danni beside him. Contrary to his calm surface, everything inside Jim seethed like a pit of snakes, each toxic emotion fighting for its dominant place; and laid over it all like pure, sweet icing covering a poisonous cake was the longing. Wanting to turn back the clock a few minutes and take the comfort she'd offered him. To hold her in his arms, to claim her as his and never let go.

But he knew now that keeping Danni in his life was as dangerous a hope as having faith in the mother he'd never met. He knew the reasons for abandonment, but all the understanding in the world didn't make him feel less unwanted—by either his birth mother, or Danni. After today he'd probably never see Annie again—and after this week he would return to his practice and his busy but emotionally empty life. And Danni had made it clear she was tired of the rollercoaster his life had become. She *enjoyed* predictability, she loved her emotional space, and he couldn't begin to imagine giving her either of those. Before long she'd leave him, return to her city life and her safe little bolthole.

"Well, I should go in." He stared at the closed gate as if it were a zone filled with unseen bombs.

Tender warm fingers touched his jaw, turned his face; the gentlest of kisses swept his mouth. "She'll love you, Jim," Danni whispered, her eyes luminous and beautiful as she kissed him again. "Everyone loves you."

Every touch stirred his senses, gave him the beauty of touch he'd always craved with a woman—but then, one of those seething snakes he had never known were inside him until Annie's first call, slithered up and covered his soul in darkness, biting her with its venom. *Yeah, everyone loves me—then they leave me.* "Yeah, everybody's best friend. Good old reliable Jim the enabler. Let's see what I can do for her, since that's my self-appointed role in life." He jerked his face out of her slackened hold, ignoring the shocked pain on her face, and leaped from the car to open the gate.

What had she done?

Danni watched him walking toward the tough,

wiry-looking woman in jeans, tank top beneath a cotton shirt, and an Akubra hat. It had to be Annie; she'd been waiting on the other side of the gate.

And Danni was sitting here in the car like a fool, watching him walk alone toward the mother he'd never known, letting him dictate the moves because she'd chosen totally the wrong time with everything in the past few days.

Why the *hell* had she told him he was an enabler within twenty-four hours of his discovery that he was adopted? Why had she withdrawn from him right between the two worst ordeals he'd ever faced, when he'd needed a friend so desperately?

What kind of person was she now, allowing him to go through this on his own, just to protect herself? *I attacked him to hide my fears and my pain. I couldn't bear for him to see me weak and wanting him.*

She closed her eyes, hating herself. *Just like my mother…*

I'm a selfish, selfish woman!

Just as everyone else in his life did, she'd protected herself, relying on his innate ability to survive, because it was what he'd always done. Giving and giving, so shocked when she'd wanted to give back—accepting the inevitable when she'd withdrawn that giving, at a time in his life when he'd needed it most.

She remembered Jim's mother's last words to her: *I'm glad you're going with him. I'm glad he has someone like you to stand by him. He's done it all alone for too long.*

Panic flared in her at the thought of what he was suffering alone. So what if her heart broke? At least she'd finally know how it felt to live…

She did it before she could talk herself out of it, jumping from the car and running after him. "Jim! *Jim!*"

He turned his face, frowning. Shading his eyes in the harsh sunlight.

She gasped as she caught up to him and grabbed his hand. "I want to meet—" She shook her head—she would *not* be a coward now—and told the truth. "I want to come with you. I want to be with you when you meet her."

His hand closed on hers. "Then come."

But his voice was warm, with that rich chuckle beneath, like a summer river again. He was smiling at her…and slowly, he lifted her hand to his mouth and kissed it.

She knew she was smiling back at him like a

complete idiot, but who cared? She felt happier than she'd been in two days. She was with Jim again, really *with* him.

Taking risks wasn't so scary when it meant he gave her that look—the look of pride in her, of— of *I'm not alone any more*.

If he didn't want her later, if she fell back to earth and broke everything inside her, the flight was worth it. She felt as if she were soaring....

"Hello. I recognise you from the shots Claire sent me. You're my son."

The rough, twanging voice was unmistakably feminine—undeniably like Jim's. Danni turned from her rapt contemplation of Jim's face to look at the woman who'd dumped him at birth.

Jim lowered their linked hands and turned to the woman who'd given birth to him, his heart pounding a sickening tattoo. "Hello. I'm Jim Haskell."

"Annie," his birth mother replied, putting her hand out—left hand, in deference to the hand that already held Danni's, he supposed. He grasped it.

It seemed ludicrous to shake hands with his own mother. One of the stranger moments in a life that, in the past few days, had begun to resemble a soap opera.

He could see some resemblance to himself in the eyes, the loose curls, and her height—he'd always been taller than the rest of his family. But her face, the same dark honey shade as his own, was closed. It was the only way to put it. There were shutters over her emotions.

There would be no tender, tearful reunion here, that was for sure.

"This your woman?" Annie asked, breaking into his thoughts.

He pulled himself together. "Danielle Morrison, this is, um, Annie. My birth mother."

Annie nodded and shook hands properly with Danni. "Pleased to meet you, Danielle."

"You, too, Annie." She sounded as off-kilter as he felt—and he was glad she'd run to him. To go through this underwhelming melodrama alone would have been too absurd.

Suddenly, all he wanted to do was leave, put this whole farce behind him and just forget the past few days had ever happened. Apart from Danni, that was; she was the only good thing to come out of everything since Annie's call.

"Why did you call me?" he asked bluntly, determined to get everything out in the open as fast as possible. "You don't look sick to me."

"I'm not." Annie made the admission without a trace of embarrassment. "I wanted to meet you. It seemed a good way to get you here."

Beside him he felt Danni stir, but she didn't speak. He was grateful for her restraint. "You could have just asked me."

Annie shrugged. "I'm not used to people doing things for me when I ask them."

After an awkward silence, in which no one seemed to know what to say, his birth mother said, "Well, I guess you want to meet your father. He's over here."

The flat statement sent Jim's emotions reeling. From his history studies, he'd expected his dad to be a station owner or jackaroo, or a someone who'd done a runner when Annie got pregnant. "My father's here?"

"Where else's he gonna be?" Annie snapped. "Come on, then, he should be on lunch break now. He's head shearer, so he hasn't got much time to waste."

She turned and strode toward an outdoor pavilion without looking to see if they followed her.

Danni squeezed his hand in silent empathy as she led him along. Dazed, he let her lead. In a week of shocks, this one was the hardest to hit.

Before he could process it, he was standing before a man sitting at the head of a long table. He was wolfing down a pie and vegetables, his concentration on his food. He looked up when Annie coughed, looking at Jim without much curiosity or even interest. "So you're Jim, eh? I'm Michael—Mick Brant."

So my real name's Jim Brant, was all he could think as he did the awkward left-hand shake again because Danni was holding his right as tightly as he was gripping it back, his only lifeline to sanity. "Um, hello, Mick."

Again, he could see the resemblance to himself and he could see that Mick, like Annie, was one of their people.

Mick nodded and smiled at Danni. "You got a pretty woman there," he remarked.

Jim performed introductions, feeling as if he'd fallen down the rabbit hole or stepped through the looking glass. He wondered if he was still asleep somewhere. This had the flat, *this could happen to me* reality to it he was always glad to awaken from.

"Guess you got some questions," Mick said, nodding. "It's a bad time right now. Can you wait till tonight? There's a dinner and shed dance. We can talk then. You know how to shear a sheep? We're a few short, and I hear you work with animals." He looked hopefully at them both.

"We can both shear," he replied, more certain every moment that he was dreaming or had taken a hallucinogenic drug without knowing it. Where were the explanations, the embarrassed apology that these two had ditched him and disappeared?

"Good." Mick pushed his chair back. "You need lunch first? You're gonna earn it. We can also give you a cabin to sleep in tonight."

Danni wrapped her free arm around the front of his waist. "Sit down, Jim. I'll get you something."

Too stunned to think of thanking her, he sat, vaguely noting Danni's swift, accusing look at the two people who had caused his life.

Mick excused himself and left for the shearing shed. Annie sat beside Jim, not moving or speaking.

He started when Danni touched his shoulder. "Eat, Jim. You need it."

He ate what she put in front of him, feeling the way he had when he'd had chicken pox at twelve: the world around him spun too slowly and yet he couldn't keep up.

Danni stood behind him, rubbing his shoulders as she had the night at his parents'.

His parents. Who the hell were his parents?

"I've got to get back to work soon," Annie said, blunt yet hesitant. "If you really want to know anything, ask now. Otherwise it'll have to wait for tonight."

His mind wiped blank at her words. He couldn't think of a thing to say.

After a long moment Danni asked, sounding hesitant, but stepping into the breach for him, "Are you and Mick still…together?" She was still holding Jim's shoulders, as if he'd fly apart if she let go.

Maybe he would. In a world where everything seemed filled with lies, cover-ups and all the wrong people, there was Danni: the one thing that was right and beautiful.

Annie frowned and nodded. "Yep." She turned and looked at Jim. "Guess you're wondering why we gave you up."

Slowly, he nodded. It seemed a good place to start.

"Mick hit the road when I had you. Couldn't handle a baby, he said." She frowned and looked down at the plastic tablecloth covering the long piece of wood on workbench ends that was the makeshift dining table. "I had no money, nowhere to go. All I knew was shearing and working the fields. I hated domestic work. I couldn't take you. I had to find Mick. I thought I'd just leave you there a few months, till Mick changed his mind—but he never did."

"He was taken, too?" Danni asked softly, kneading his knotted muscles with a sure, gentle touch.

"Stolen, you mean," Annie retorted, her voice filled with quiet hate. "Yeah, we both were. I don't want to talk about it." She tensed. "Doesn't do any good. I met Mick when I was seventeen. I ran away from the foster place they sent me to be with him. Cops came and took me back, but I ran again—and this time they couldn't find us," she said with pride ringing in her voice. "We got on the shearing route, and we've been on it ever since. Not too many of us left, but Mick and me, we love the life."

"You…never had more children?" Danni asked again, and Jim was grateful. He couldn't *think* enough to ask anything.

"Oh, yeah," Annie said, her tone offhand. "Years later. Another boy and a girl. Mick was okay by then, we had good work shearing and fruit picking, so we took them with us. Sean's nineteen, and a jackaroo out east. Jackie, she's twenty-one, married to a bloke in Tamworth, got her own baby now. A boy, Blake."

I have a brother and sister, even a nephew. Oh, it got better and better.

"Why didn't you ever come to see me. Take me back?" he asked, through numb lips.

Annie shifted on her seat. "I rang when you were about eight, and again when you were fifteen. Both times, Bob and Claire said you didn't know about me—that you were happy. You were happy there, weren't you?" she demanded.

Thrown into acute discomfort, he nodded. He'd had a good childhood, all things considered. Bob and Claire couldn't have been more loving parents. They never had much, but everything was shared with family love and laughter.

"You had a better childhood than me. You got to stay with your family. You had schooling, brothers and sisters, and a good home life."

Put that way, Jim felt stupid, selfish. He no longer knew how to accuse her of anything.

"I think Jim's wondering why you kept the other children, and not him," Danni said gently.

"It's a natural enough thing to wonder, don't you think?"

He leaned back against her. Brave, beautiful, taking risk after risk for his sake. Was it any wonder he loved this woman?

"I told you. We had no money, no home. Mick took off—I had to find him. I did the best I could in giving you to Claire!" Annie's voice was harsh, belligerent but vulnerable. "I travelled a week to get you there. You said you were happy. You have a good life now, right?"

He frowned, and slowly nodded. Seen through Annie's eyes, somehow he *did* understand. It wasn't that she didn't care; she'd just put Mick first because he was all she'd had. Never having been raised by a loving family, she hadn't known what to do with a baby except to repeat the sad history that had happened with her, and Mick: to give it away.

Not *him*, just—a baby.

Yes, it was history repeating itself, but he'd had a happy ending.

Had he really suffered? Bob and Claire hadn't had much, but he'd have had less with Mick and Annie. Bob and Claire—*Mum and Dad*—had given him all they could. He'd had five younger brothers and sisters to love and care for. He'd been a needed part of their lives. He'd gone to the selective high school, and to university, with their blessing and what financial support they could give. They'd been there for every milestone in his life. So had almost everyone else in the family.

It seemed everyone's choices had made him the man he was—and he was happy with the person he was. Maybe being dumped was the best thing that had ever happened to him.

So what *was* he complaining about?

He almost laughed. This had to rank as the most absurd day of his life, yet it was the day he'd discovered himself and found that wasn't so bad a place to be.

"I do have a good life," he said, quashing a mad desire to thank her for ditching him.

"Well, then, let's get shearing." Annie shoved her chair back, much as Mick had done, and walked out of the pavilion toward the shed without looking back.

"You okay?" Danni whispered in his ear, her voice tender.

Needing her so much it hurt, he turned his face. With a smile, she leaned in and kissed him, brief and beautiful in its *feeling*. A sweet anchor in the strange storm his life had become in the past week.

He still didn't know why Annie and Mick had asked him to come, but he had a feeling they were saving the best until last.

CHAPTER NINE

DINNER WAS PAST, AND THE DANCE in full swing, and still Annie and Mick hadn't shown.

Knowing he needed the distraction, as she did from her hunger—because dinner was mostly steak and sausages, she'd had limp salad, bread and butter and rice salad—Danni dragged Jim onto the dance floor and endured one boot-scootin' tune after another. Her eyes were blurry with exhaustion from shearing, feet were killing her and her head throbbed with the excess of bass on the speakers; but she kept pretending she wanted to dance, keeping him busy until they decided to show their faces.

She turned down every offer to dance from the excess of single men, keeping her hand in Jim's. And all the while, she watched the door.

Almost two hours into the dance, Jim's birth parents entered the cleared barn that was the dance hall tonight. It only took them seconds to find their son—he was easily the tallest in the room—and Mick cocked his head.

"Here we go," Jim murmured, having been watching the door as often as she had. "I guess I'm about to find out what they want. You want to stay here and party?"

Seeing that look on his face again—the neutral face hiding the seething mass of emotion he didn't yet know how to handle—she shot him a mock-darkling look. "With this motley lot of single men panting for female attention? You're not going anywhere without me." She shoved her hand back in his, clinging hard.

He chuckled, as she'd hoped he would, and led her out of the barn.

Annie and Mick were waiting for them outside the door. Unlike Claire and Bob, they didn't chafe at Danni's presence; they either accepted her as Jim's woman, or they didn't care enough for Jim's opinion to worry about talking private business before a stranger.

Jim's a stranger to them, too.

Sadness filled her soul. Open-hearted, giving Jim should never have had this crazy life tossed in his lap; but who ever said life was fair?

"I suppose you're wondering why we asked you here," Mick began, his face and voice calm and confident.

"Besides wanting to meet our son, of course," Annie added, with the first touch of anxiety Danni had seen in her.

Jim said quietly, "It's okay, Annie. No offence, but it's obvious meeting me wasn't your most important agenda, or you'd have made some time for me before ten at night."

"Nice big words," Mick said sneering. "Learn them at that fancy school you went to?"

Jim lifted his chin. "Don't throw my education at me. I can't help the life you gave me any more than you can help what happened to you."

Danni squeezed his hand. She wanted to cheer him on.

Annie jumped in. "Mick, stop it. He's right." She looked Jim in the eye. "We're getting too old for the wandering life. We'd like to settle somewhere near Jackie, but we need help. A deposit for a little house—in the cheaper area outside Tamworth," she added, her anxiety now obvious.

"You've got the money—you own your practice," Mick added, his face pugnacious and yet heartbreaking because it was an older version of Jim's. But where Jim was open to the world, Mick expected only rejection.

Mick is what Jim would have become, had he never been given to his adoptive family, if he'd been forced to live the wandering life.

"You can afford to help us out," Mick snapped when Jim didn't jump in with an offer. "You got your fancy life because of us. You have advantages Sean and Jackie never did."

Jim's brow lifted. "Because you ditched me and kept the other two, you mean?"

Mick didn't even flinch. His eyes were hard. "You got a problem with your life? When did Bob and Claire beat you, or shuffle you off to the next place when they couldn't be bothered with you?"

Jim took a step forward, a mirror image of his father in his belligerence. "Are you saying that happened to Sean and Jackie?"

"That's none of your business." Mick snarled.

"And that's the point, isn't it? Your kids are none of my business, because I don't know them. I don't know you either. Your financial needs are none of my business any more than your kids are. And for your information, I sank everything I have into the practice. I have no more money, except what I earn."

"So take out a loan. Banks will let *you* in the door—but me, a man who's worked every day of my life since I was fourteen, I'm a *security risk*." Mick snapped his fingers. "You take a loan out for that big, shiny car you got?"

"I don't have to justify my life or car to you." He held his birth father's gaze. "What I have, I got through hard work. I got into the selective school and the university scholarship on my own, and worked at a steak house for years to pay for my room and board." He didn't sound furious; he didn't sound calm, either, but something between. *Honest.* "Neither of you lifted a finger for me in thirty years, or even bothered to come to see me. Bob Haskell is my father, and he's been the best dad I could have asked for. Claire is my mother. If they need my help, they get it, no questions asked. They deserve it." He turned away. "You are strangers—the people who dumped me with my real parents."

Danni almost burst with the pride and love she felt for him. Being Jim, she had no doubt he'd help them later—but with his words, he'd established a pattern of respect Annie and Mick would have to follow from now on.

The days of Jim the enabler had gone, if they'd ever existed.

His birth parents stared at him for a moment; then Mick turned his back and walked off without a word.

Annie gave him a long look. "You think we were rough on you, do you? You got no idea, boy. You weren't put in a home for boys that only *bad* kids went to, and sent out to foster homes to be an unpaid servant. You were loved and cared for all your life. Just go ask Sean or Jackie what life's been like out here, what life's like for people like us. We've worked for everything all our lives—and everything don't amount to more than what's in our cabin. We just wanted a leg up, for once. Nothing you couldn't afford."

She turned her back as Mick had and walked away.

Danni hardly dared to look at Jim when they were alone. She just stood there holding his hand, wondering what he was thinking, feeling.

If it had been her, she'd be hating all her parents right now, and the whole damn world. Using her pain as a reason to withdraw from life and nurse her bitterness until she felt safe and strong again.

"They're right, you know," he murmured eventually, his voice quiet, reflective. "I've got no idea what my life would have been like if I'd stayed with them. I'd probably be a shearer or jackaroo, or on welfare, if they hadn't given me to Mum and Dad."

Danni all but gaped at him. "You're okay about this?"

All her life, she'd believed that to forgive meant to lose power, to put herself in a weaker position; but Jim didn't appear beaten. He seemed more thoughtful than angry.

"I expected something like this," he said, breaking into her thoughts with the confirmation. "After all, I must be a big success in their eyes, and if they didn't bring me here to brag to their friends about their son the vet—and they didn't introduce us to anyone—it had to be for money."

He didn't even sound bitter…either about Annie and Mick, or his adoptive parents. Was there no end to the strength of this gentle man?

Moved, half-afraid, she turned to him, wrapping her arms around his waist. "That you turned out so well is no credit to them, Jim. You owe them nothing. You didn't choose to be conceived, or to be adopted."

"I guess I'm not even adopted." He shrugged, his arms sliding round her as naturally as if they belonged there. "But there must be some of them in me. I don't know what their lives were like. They did the best they could at the time. They can't have been more than nineteen or twenty when they had me."

She frowned up at him. "You're going to do it, aren't you? You'll give them their deposit."

"Maybe." He rubbed his cheek against her hair. "I'll see what I can do. All my capital's tied up in the practice. I rent my house in Cooinda, and already have a loan for the car."

She linked her hands together behind his back to hide their shaking. Give, give and give again; he never stopped, yet never seemed to run out of strength or love.

"Can you really be as good about this as you seem?" she wondered aloud. "You've had the worst week of your life. You can't have come to terms with it already."

"I guess the truth has freed me," he said quietly. "I don't mean this won't backlash on me one day—it probably will. There's still anger and humiliation, deep down. But at least I know where I am now—I know who I am. I know

Mum and Dad really wanted me. They never treated me as anything less than their own child."

"The truth didn't free you," she mumbled, forcing the words out because she needed to say it, because she was shamed by his strength. "Your forgiveness did." She lifted her gaze to his, knowing her eyes were stinging again. "I've never had that—*gift*. I always thought that if I forgave someone, it was leverage for them to hurt me over and over."

"I suppose it is, for some people." He nuzzled her cheek with his lips. "But what they do with my forgiveness is their problem. I don't have to make it mine. If they do it again, I can choose to be hurt and angry, or I can pity them. If they're that toxic, they can't be happy. Either way, it doesn't belong to me."

She couldn't understand him, couldn't fathom his ability to constantly reach out to people who didn't deserve it—but oh, how she wanted to. She wanted to stay by his side, remain in his life until she knew how to be like him, for it seemed he held the key to a simple happiness in living she'd never found.

No more denial—she had nowhere else to go but to the truth. She loved him, adored him, and wanted to become the kind of woman he could be proud of.

If only I could—but miracles don't happen to people like me.

He was still moving his lips across her cheek. She turned her face and kissed him with all the beautiful turbulence in her soul. He lifted her up, gathering her so close she flowed right into him, part of his body, kissing her back with all his giving nature.

This was *real;* and this kiss, the moment, slipped inside her unconscious, opening her locked and guarded heart and took the key away, putting it in Jim's pocket.

"You asked how I could be okay," he mumbled between kisses, sleepy passion in his eyes. "*This* is why. *You.* You wouldn't have come to me without everything that happened, would you, Danni?"

It was an excellent question. She shook her head, smiling ruefully at the realisation she'd just made. Hiding behind her barriers had done nothing to make her safe against what this man could do to her.

"I don't know how I'd be now if you hadn't come with me—if you hadn't told me, *shown* me how much you want me. I've waited all my life for a woman like you. You've been my rock, my strength since this began. I wouldn't have gotten through all this but for you, watching you step out from behind all your legitimate fears for me, only to help me. You say you're unable to give, but it's all you've done for me since that night in Bathurst."

He'd punctuated the words with kisses, each one like a tiny drop of healing in her heart, warming her numb, cold soul. *Jim needed her.*

"I've made mistakes, Jim. I've held back."

"So have I." He kissed her again and again. "This thing between us is so *intense,* it's frightening."

"I wouldn't have done it for anyone else," she mumbled, kissing him back, feeling beautiful and aching with arousal. "I always wanted you, *always.*"

"Ah, Danni-girl," he muttered, hoarse with desire, and took the kiss deeper, until she could think of nothing but what he was doing to her: bringing her to life, after years in a kind of suspended animation. She wanted him so much….

Panting, she pulled back, wishing she could say the words, *Come to bed. Come and live with me and be my lover*. But she still needed safety, needed a guarantee. She needed him to see the kind of person she could become.

He had to meet her mother and father first.

"So…you're going to help Annie and Mick?" Her voice was breathless, trembling with the strength and depth of her desire.

He nuzzled her throat. "I can't commit yet. I might need to take out another loan to do it. If they had a deposit, the bank should give them a loan—especially if I'm their guarantor." His voice was thoughtful, calculating dollars and cents. Ready to give them away.

"How many of your brothers' and sisters' courses have you paid for?" she asked, knowing he'd done it. "How big a debt are you carrying for your family?"

Jim grinned and kissed her. "Nothing I can't afford. I'm earning good money now, and paying it back. All my family needed was a start. They're doing fine on their own now."

"They needed a start—and an example to follow." Wishing she'd had a brother or sister to help and guide. Then she might not be the screwed-up mess she was now. Then again, that child might be even more mixed up than she was.

The grin vanished. "I am what I am, Danni. Keeping all my good things to myself wouldn't make me happy. Not helping out when friends and family call me would destroy something inside me. If that makes me an enabler, so be it."

She looked down. "You're not, Jim—not even close. I said that because I needed to believe it. If I didn't have to respect you, and all you do, I could keep my life to myself without feeling selfish and weak."

"Without letting me in."

"Yes," she whispered, needing options still. Needing a bolthole.

A finger lifted her chin, gentle but remorseless. "And now?"

A sudden wildness filled her soul at the fire in his eyes. "And now—you're you, and I'm me. I don't think I can change either."

His smile was sure. "I don't want you to change. The woman you are is the one I want. Don't you know that yet?"

She bit her lip hard and shook her head. "You deserve better." Her voice grated, trying to push past the lump in her throat.

Bending, he brushed her mouth with his, over

and over, until her teeth released her lip, her arms were wound tight around his neck and she was kissing him back with years of pent-up passion. "Can I deserve you?" he murmured against her mouth.

Passion died. She stared up at him, so unsure, so afraid. "For how long?"

His face darkened, but not in anger. "I'm not your father."

She closed her eyes to stop the stinging. She hadn't cried since she was eight, and *damned* if she'd start now. She wouldn't use weapons on him to get him to stay. "I know what I am, Jim. I've pushed everyone away all my life. I don't know how to have faith."

"I'll teach you." He touched her cheek. "We all have baggage, Danni-girl. I'm good at believing, so we balance out."

I can't believe. I can't begin to believe you'll stay.

After she'd gulped and gulped again, she gave up trying to get rid of the pain in her throat. "Can we take this one day at a time?"

He took her face in his hands. "No one else. Just you and me."

It wasn't a question; it was a demand, and a

wave of joy so strong it *hurt* washed through her. "I don't want anyone else. Just you."

She gasped as soft kisses feathered up her throat. "Say it again."

Her head fell back, taking in the kisses like balm to her wounded soul. "I want you, Jim. Only you." It was an easy thing to say—the thought of any other man touching her this way, giving her such beauty and happiness, was impossible to contemplate.

"No more hiding or denial."

"No, no," she whispered, threading her hands through his hair, pulling him around to kiss his mouth. "That was for you. You needed time."

"So did you," he mumbled between kisses.

Her heart jerked at his knowledge of her. So many years of hiding, but he stripped walls she'd spent decades building, and seemed to do it with ease. "I'm still afraid…."

He almost crushed her in his grip. "You're not alone in that. But I won't let you run again, Danni. You're my woman."

Her heart melted at the demand cloaked in rough, vulnerable honesty. "I still need time." Just until he met her parents. Just until then. She had to believe in him if he still wanted her then, surely?

He groaned into her neck. "You mean we can't make love tonight?"

Shivering in longing, she whispered, "This is the biggest risk I've taken in my life." She pulled back to gaze up at him. "Please. Just give me a little more time."

"What? You want *more* time after I've given you, what, four whole days?"

At the laughing, rueful words, she glanced up at him…and his slow smile of tenderness warmed her right through. "You have the cabin," he whispered. "I'll set up the tent."

"I think we should leave here," she said, breathless yet serious. "It's not healthy."

"For whom?" he asked, kissing her jaw. Melting her from the inside out, shaking her resolution with a single touch.

She almost said it—*for you*—because there was no way he could really be okay about this situation with Annie and Mick; but she couldn't make her mouth work. She couldn't be such a hypocrite, judging him by her own pathetic standards of self-healing.

And he was kissing down her throat again…. Oh, what he was *doing* to her wiped her mind and mouth clean of words.

"What? I—can't—oh, *Jim*…" She clung to him.

With one last, deep kiss on her shoulder, he looked up. His sleepy-eyed gaze on her was too hot, too knowing. "We stay here tonight, Danni, because I can't answer for my actions if I'm alone with you in a car right now—and I don't think you'll want to stop me."

Hot shivers raced through her. "No," she admitted, with a tiny gulp. "I wouldn't." If he took her to that bed now, she would give him all he asked, and more.

But slowly, he shook his head. "I won't give you any reason to hide from me."

The stark words, harsh with desire, showed how much he respected her. If he didn't, he'd have kept kissing her until she was too blind and besotted with passion to remember her fears or her past.

She closed her eyes and said the words in her heart. Or some of them. "I know I can trust you."

"But you don't, not yet, or we'd be in that bed right now. I'll wait until you're ready to believe I won't leave you." His voice was gravel-rough now, hard and wanting. "You might be the death of me—but I can wait, because I've never felt so alive with a woman before." He drew back and looked down at her, his eyes dark, lush, beautiful. "I love you, Danni."

She gasped; her mind reeled. Why, *why* had he said that, within two minutes of agreeing to give her time? It—it wasn't as if he could actually *mean* it. "No," she whispered, her breathing fast and shallow. "I—I don't believe it. You—you're vulnerable after your parents… It's not t-true. You *can't* love me."

He held her close. "Breathe deeper, Danni, or you'll pass out. Come on, baby, in…out. In…out. Slow it down. That's it. Good." His voice was low, soothing. "Now what's this nonsense about? You think I said it because my parents deserted me thirty years ago, and I've had a happy life since?" He smiled at her, warm, intimate. "I'm not tragic, Danni."

She blinked, her thoughts scrambling. "But—after all you've just been through—"

"All *I've* been through? Not me, Danni. Feel sorry for Annie and Mick."

She gulped down, hard. "But—it's natural to want someone to love, to belong to. You feel lost. After being let down and hurt by those who should have loved and nurtured you…"

"Is that one of your life rules, Danni? If that's

true, then you've had, what, a couple of lovers in your life? Or is it more? I remember all the guys you hit on through the years, thinking you were madly in love…right?"

Her earnest words withered and died on her lips. He was right. She *hadn't* acted that way, never once since high school. "But…" She sighed and shook her head.

"But what, Danni? Come on, baby, I'm not the one feeling lost here. So just say what's on your mind." When her head fell, so afraid to say it out loud, he said grimly, "Laila? Is she part of the problem?"

No! But she couldn't deny it, even to say *No— it's about me. No man can love me for long.* She hiccupped, once, twice and again, wishing she knew how to reconstruct her barriers—to re-learn how to not *care* so damn much.

He kept up his rhythmic stroking of her back, using the heel of his palm. When her hiccups slowed to one every minute, he spoke. "Danni, I love Laila to bits, but she was right all along. It was brother-sister love. I've known that since I left Wallaby Station three years ago, and saw how she and Jake were with each other. I felt sad at losing her, but it wasn't the kind of sadness I expected it to be. It was more lonely—like I wanted someone of my own. I still called it love, because I didn't know any different. Because though I knew you, I didn't *have* you. I didn't know what was here for us until I touched you." He lifted her face. "Don't you think I'd have fought for Laila any time during those seven years, if I'd truly loved her?"

Taken aback by the rightness of all he said, she stuttered, "I—I thought y-you…"

"Danni, look at the difference in me with Laila, and with you." His voice was strong, sure. "I let Laila have her way with it all those years—but from the first night I've been fighting for you. It can only mean one thing. I never really loved her that way at all."

She frowned, remembering her smugness that first night. Laila had never made Jim *feel* so much, or yes, he'd have fought back. The caveman in him came out without warning with her, Danni—and just as swiftly came the tenderness.

He admitted now, without a trace of pain, "When I saw her with Jake—so alive and vivid and strong, fighting for him—I knew she'd never felt like that about me…and I had to admit I'd never felt about her the way Jake did." His eyes grew intense. "Like I'd kill the man who tried to take my woman from me. Like I'd move heaven and earth to keep her with me for life. I'd never felt that way about any woman, until the day I got that sleaze off you. I said I was doing a good deed—but I *hated* the way he touched you. I wanted to belt the mongrel into tomorrow, but I had to put your future first. So I did it the other way—but touching you…the *intensity* of it, coming so sudden, scared the hell out of me. So I walked away, and I wish to hell I hadn't, because now you don't believe I'm not going to walk away again. You don't believe I love you. But I'm not going anywhere, Danni. I told you the first night I'd fight for you, and I will. I'll fight for the right to stand beside you for the rest of my life."

Her head was swimming now. A mixture of fierce gladness, complete disbelief and utter terror filled her, and for the life of her she couldn't work out which was uppermost. "You need stability after the past few days, someone who can't change on you, and I'm the only candidate…."

He touched her forehead with his, smiling. "Do I seem weak or scared to you? Is it me who feels vulnerable, Danni? I know this is rotten timing, but I *know* what I feel."

A quiver ran all the way through her. Oh, how she *wanted* to believe that, but she'd been on best behaviour for days, reaching out and giving... being someone she wasn't for his sake. She couldn't guarantee its lasting...so how could his feelings for her be real? "Jim, I don't feel *safe*—"

"I don't feel safe with you either, Danni," he said softly. "It's not just physical, and it's not a comfortable thing either, like it was with Laila. It's bloody frightening, how much I feel for you. You can get me mad so fast my head spins, you make me want you and almost hate you—but when I'm with you I'm *alive*. Like I've been born over again with a new skin. You challenge me, make me think in ways I've never had to. You strip all my defences, make me see myself through new eyes—but I wouldn't have it any other way."

A perfect summing up: *you strip my defences*. And Jim might be comfortable with that, but she wasn't—far from it. Every word he spoke terrified her more, yet she didn't want to pull away and run into the darkness, where she'd be alone again.

Alone had always meant safety to her before.

Now it meant cold emptiness, a world without Jim's warmth and giving and a smile that brought her to life, a touch that melted her barricades, and she didn't care; but *alone* was the only place she'd ever truly *belonged*.

It was time to go back.

She couldn't look at him. "Jim...I can't do this."

A lively country song floated out from the barn, covering the silence and yet making it stronger. At this moment, Danni wished she could go back to half an hour before, and take her chances with the desperate and dateless inside the barn—*anything* rather than seeing the sad comprehension in his eyes.

"You don't just mean now, do you?" he asked quietly.

Her eyes stung and burned again, bringing on a headache. "I'm—"

"Don't say *sorry*, Danni. Just don't! And for God's sake don't cry!"

The fierce growl startled her. She bit her lip. "I don't know what else to say."

The warm current of summer night air felt like a wintry slap as he released her. "You said only ten minutes ago we were together."

What could she say to that? "That was before…" *Before you said the fatal three words.*

Hearing them was shocking enough; believing in them was another. Only four days ago she'd been certain he loved another woman. Only two days ago—two *hours* ago—she'd been convinced love and happy-ever-after would never be hers—and *never* with a man as incredible as Jim.

And that was it; the worst truth lying in her heart. *I don't believe you love me. You can't love me.*

She couldn't say it. She'd hurt him enough.

He picked up some rocks around their feet and began throwing them at the wooden posts that were the paddock fence, his face like thunder in the light of several fire torches the owners had used to light the way to the cabins. "I won't ask if you love me. If you do, you're not ready to admit it, and if you think you don't, I refuse to hear it."

Something in her ached and burned: a reflection of the pain she'd caused him. Wishing that he hadn't chosen tonight of all nights to say this, and make her reject him. He'd endured more than enough rejection for one night. "It's not that I don't *feel* something for you. I do. I just don't know what name to give it, if it's real, or it's going to last." On unsteady legs, she walked over to the paddock fence, leaning on it as if it were a lifeline. "I've never known what love is, Jim."

Peering at him over her arms as she leaned her chin there, she saw his hand open and slowly drop the rest of the rocks he'd been ready to throw. He muttered something, paced toward her and back again, and sighed. "Except for the kind of humiliation and ridicule you heard every day from your parents—and that isn't love, it's unhealthy obsession. No wonder you're so damned scared of love, with those two as an example."

Startled anew, she turned her face, a hundred questions in her heart.

As if hearing them, he nodded. "I've heard them. After I helped you lose the sleaze at graduation, I went outside. They were going at each other over who had more time with you, among other things."

She drew in a shuddering breath. "I don't want to know what *other things* were."

"It wasn't important." He touched her shoulder. "Go and rest. You need time to sort everything out in your head. You told me that," he said wryly, "and I rushed it, in my worst imitation of a bull at a fence."

She nodded, and began heading for the cluster of shearers' sheds.

"I'll camp right outside the cabin." He cocked his head at the barn, and the shearers and jackaroos stumbling from the spill of light toward them. "You don't need any company tonight. Not even mine." He gave her a crooked grin and winked.

The pain became unbearable at his consideration and caring, when she'd just rejected his love. "I don't want to lose you," she blurted.

His whole face softened. "If you don't love me, Danni, you're giving a damned fine imitation of it."

It was as if he'd put cold chains over her soul with the words. "Don't put words in my mouth, Haskell. Don't push me. I'll say them myself, if and when I feel them—and when I'm good and ready."

"One day at a time, remember?" Another wry smile. "Or maybe it's me that needs to remember. After years of waiting for the wrong woman, I want my life with the right one to start right here and now…but you need time to see I'm here for life."

Instead of feeling reassured, her heart and soul darkened. "What if you get tired of waiting for me?" But what she was really thinking was *What if you don't really love me, either? What if I give my life to you and you find out I'm the wrong woman, too?*

Oh, *God*, it would kill her.

"I can't promise I won't." He came toward her, slow and sure, and touched her face. "But I'll tell you first. One day at a time, Danni. I know you want me to be with you when you face your parents—and then, I'll go home. You can be free—have time to think. But know this—I won't just get tired and disappear. I won't let you go without a hell of a fight."

A *fight*? She buried her face in his chest. All he ever had to do was put his hand out to her, and she put hers in it; smile at her, touch her, and her doubts and fears became beauty and vivid, living certainty.

But could it last? To love him and lose him would force her to live in the bitter emptiness of her mother.

Jim was a man in a lifetime, an honest and beautiful miracle she knew could never be repeated. If she threw him away from fear—

"You're shaking," he whispered, and enveloped her in warm, strong arms. But with a tiny cry, she broke away and bolted to the safety of her cabin, dodging cheerful drunks on the way, not stopping until she'd locked the door behind herself.

But the cabin was dark and empty. The shelter it provided was only physical—and she didn't want to be alone anymore.

Then what do you want?

The lump in her throat turned hard and sharp; swallowing only made the pain worse.

Giving up the fight, she buried her face in her hands and, for the first time in more than twenty years, she allowed the tears to come.

CHAPTER TEN

THE CRASHING STORM SOUNDS of one of her parents calling happened for the fifth time the next day—and Jim wanted to hit something. Every single day they called twice, three times—always separately—saying the same thing they'd said a hundred times. He marvelled at Danni's patience with them; but he *hated* the look on her face after she hung up.

The fire in her eyes, not of sweet passion, but the need to run—yet she was all they had, and Danni never shirked responsibility.

He wondered if she realised that was why they called so often: insecurity. Because they knew she saw them as her responsibility, and they wanted her love, even if they didn't always deserve it.

He'd tell her, one day…whether they worked things out or not. It was his nature, he thought wryly. The worry would eat at him until he'd at least tried to fix it for her.

He turned down the CD player as Danni answered with a sigh. "Hi, Dad. Fine, thanks, and how are you both? Good. Yes, we're on our way, but we won't make it past the Hunter Valley today—the western edge. We'll be there by dinner tomorrow night." She listened for a few moments, her face closing off. "Dad, can we just leave that? I really don't want to talk about it. It's really not your business until I tell you," she added in sudden anger. "I am a twenty-nine-year-old woman and my life is my own."

Jim wanted to sigh. Obviously her dad had asked for another status update on their relationship. Every day one of her parents asked it—as if a day could undo all the damage they'd done to her with the marriage that should never have happened.

Anxious to see her happy, probably terrified it was their fault that she'd been closed off from the normal joys of finding someone for so many years...

A wave of pity filled him for the people who obviously had no life apart from their only child. He wanted to snatch the phone from Danni and say *It's okay, I love her and I'm not going anywhere. I already make her happy. She just needs time to believe in me.*

And he'd say it at this moment, if he thought Danni would forgive him for sharing her deepest fears with the two people who'd instigated them.

She sat ramrod straight when she flipped the phone shut, her eyes staring ahead with the blindness of imperfectly hidden distress.

Gently he took the phone from her and switched it off. "Problem solved for a few hours. Want to drive?"

She turned to him, but didn't see him. "Why?"

He shrugged and pulled over to the side of the road. "I find the concentration works off the anger, and clears my head."

Unbuckling her seatbelt was her only answer.

After an hour he gave up trying to sleep, but didn't bother talking to her. Two days of silence was getting hard to handle; but hearing Danni's pain during every phone call, the fear she tried so hard to keep buried deep inside, his heart melted anew. She must be terrified of going home to more of the same.

This was *not* the time to push his wants onto her.

"Say something, damn it," she said out of the

blue. "I know you're awake. I can hear your brain ticking over, wondering what to say to me. Just blurt it out and get it over with!"

So aggressive, hiding her terror. So vulnerable beneath her prickles. "I don't think I'm qualified to comment on the state of your family right now," he said with deliberate dryness.

"But you still want to." It wasn't a question.

"It doesn't always matter what I want, does it? This week's been a good time for me to realise I can't fix everything for everyone."

"Even when someone's asking you?" she said softly.

He turned to her, searching her face. "Are you asking?"

With a little shrug that conveyed a world of tiredness, she sighed. "Nothing I've tried through the years has helped. I can't keep running, either."

Joy streaked through him. Danni was moving out of her comfort zone, ready to share her deepest-held pain and fear—and she was doing it voluntarily. "I had one of those deep and meaningful friends in high school. She loved poetry and pretty cards and letters. She taught me The Serenity Prayer—do you know it?"

She frowned and nodded. "Don't they teach that at AA meetings?"

"At most meetings of people who need new coping skills," he agreed. "Right now, I think the first line is applicable to your relationship with your parents."

After a deep silence, she repeated it. "God, grant me the serenity to accept the things I cannot change." She sucked in her top lip. "All my life I've tried to accept how they are, but deep down, I kept on wanting change. That's not acceptance."

"You were trying to find normality," he suggested.

"Yes. All my life I've wanted to be like everyone else—but it always felt as if there was some massive barrier, like an ocean I couldn't cross."

He touched her hand on the steering wheel. "I was always the outsider from the time I went to the selective high school, only one of two Aboriginal kids there. I always felt that barrier, but once I accepted I couldn't make it go away, it somehow didn't matter so much."

Turning her hand, she linked her fingers through his. "Why do you bother with me?" Her voice was low, trembling with repressed emotion.

He lifted her hand to his and kissed it. "You know the answer to that."

"No...*why?* How can you think you love me?" she burst out. "I'm not lovable, Jim. I know what I am, full of defences and anger. I'm a loner, an outsider. Being in my life will always be hard work."

Though she didn't phrase it as a question, he heard it beneath, and his heart, already melted, bubbled over with love and compassion for the girl who was so afraid to reach out, she never knew her capacity to give was so enormous, and the woman who still didn't know how amazing she was to him. "When my life fell apart, who was there for me?"

After a long silence she said, in almost a whisper, "Me."

"When my parents tried to get rid of you, why did you stay?"

"Be-because you needed me." She sounded confused.

He nodded. "Yes, because I needed you, Danni."

She shrugged. "That was just a day. Anyone can reach out for a day."

"When you could have gone home, why did you stay with me?"

Her fingers gripped his harder. "Don't, Jim. I'm no heroine. I just wanted to be with you." She sighed. "To take what I could get with you before you got tired of me and gave me a sweet goodbye."

"You say it was selfish, yet you stood by me when I met Annie and Mick. When I couldn't ask the questions, you did it for me—and you even turned down the attention of fifty other single men for me," he ended on a teasing note to break her tension.

She gave a little laugh. "That was no hardship."

"You came after me when I gave you every excuse to leave me alone when I met Annie."

"I was ashamed." She snatched her hand out of his, gripping the steering wheel as if it would save her life.

"Of what?" he asked gently and held his breath. If she told him—

"So stupid," she mumbled still, her face white. "She called, and I couldn't stand it. *My best friend!* I know you said it's over, and I shouldn't resent how much you love her now, but I've never been loved like that. And all those years she had her family, and she had you…"

"Were you always jealous of how I felt about her?" He barely breathed. Danni thought she didn't know how to reach out, but she was touching his soul without even realising it.

"Yes, all right? *Yes*," she snapped. "I wanted you the first day I saw you, and you were with her all the time, fussing over her like she was so damn fragile. It annoyed the *hell* out of me. Laila had always been loved and fussed over, and you did it over again! She said she didn't want to be a princess."

"She doesn't, Danni," he said softly. "All she ever wanted was to be loved."

"Yeah, well, some people are a living example of the haves getting more, and the have-nots getting nothing!"

"Danni—"

"Oh, no!" she cried suddenly and swerved the car.

A country boy, he knew what it meant. He shot his glance to the windscreen and the road beyond—and saw the waddling wombat she was trying to avoid.

But as she swerved to the left, a massive tree loomed in front of them…*in front of him*.

He grabbed the wheel and turned it back toward the road, knowing the wombat couldn't possibly move fast enough to get out of the way.

The sickening up-down thuds beneath the four-wheel drive told a story he'd lived twenty times during his adult life, and hundreds of times as a vet.

Danni turned to him, her face a new species in horrified fury. "You ran over the wombat! You did it deliberately…"

"No time for argument." He unbuckled his belt. "Get my kit. The wombat has a chance. I'd be dead now if we'd hit the tree."

She was pale as she came around to the back of the car, yanking out his bag while he checked the wombat's spine. "Is it all right?"

"Well, he's snarling pretty well," he said as he finished with the spine, moving onto the creature's legs. "I think I've broken his leg. I'll need anaesthetic, and splints and a bandage. He's a big boy, so give me the heavy-duty stuff. And call WIRES for the nearest vet hospital. He needs an X-ray."

She laid out the equipment he would need, including antiseptic wash to deal with the deep cuts before calling the injured wildlife rescue service.

"Mudgee has a vet willing to take him. We're only an hour from there," she reported after she hung up.

"Good." He'd already knocked the creature

out. "He's sleeping now. Put the splint on the inside, and the right side. I'm going to use two in case it's a spiral fracture."

She placed the splints in the exact place. "I'm so sorry, boy," she crooned. "We'll make you better soon."

"You didn't hit him. I did," he said as he worked out the best bandage size to use.

"I should have hit him. We both know that," she muttered, "but I couldn't bring myself to do it."

"You had a one-second decision to make, and you chose to save life."

"I could have killed *you*," she cried. "I could have killed you, Jim!"

"I'm alive, Danni," he said quietly, "But this wombat's in pain, and you're shaking the splint right off him. I need to check for internal injuries right now if he's going to live. I need your help."

"I'm sorry." As he'd expected, the severity pulled her together; the vet overtook the woman, and she replaced the splint in its proper place.

When they'd done the best they could to repair his injuries, Jim said, "He's in shock. He needs rest and quiet, and the fluids pushed through. Do you want to drive, or watch him and monitor his drip while I get him to Mudgee?"

"I'd rather watch him," she said as she helped lift the animal onto a towel they were using as a makeshift gurney. "I'm not up for driving now."

"Hitting wildlife is a fact of life out here. In the outback, cars are the foreign bodies, and they cause death or injury all the time."

"That happens all the time in the city, too." Her voice was shaky. "My dog got run over when I was nine—a little dachshund. He died before we could even lift him up. I *hated* seeing Brucie's eyes all glazed and the blood coming from his head."

He didn't need to ask if that was the other reason she'd become a vet. He'd been the kid who'd brought home injured wildlife wherever he found them, and doctored them back to health if he could. "Funny, isn't it?" He laid half the back seat down to make a bed large enough for the wombat. "We seem to come at things from opposite ends of the spectrum, but we reach the same conclusions in the end."

"I suppose we are alike—at times, anyway." She gave him a half shy, half ironic smile, then strapped herself in beside the wombat, checking the fluid levels of the IV.

She needed to retreat now, to gather her thoughts. These life-and-death decisions always left him shaking and needing time out to think about life.

He closed the back doors and hopped into the driver's seat.

They made it to Mudgee an hour before sundown. The vet was waiting for them and hailed them as equals, giving Jim, the country vet, the greater attention and respect.

The inference was obvious to Danni: *why aren't you working where you're needed?*

Outback medicine of any kind was a vocation. The life was tough and the people tougher. The isolation of being the only one of your kind for hundreds of kilometres, the endless hours of nothing but work, and makeshift entertainment, always on call—

How is that different to my life now?

She knew Jim had never considered working anywhere else; and for the first time, she wondered…She spent her life in her apartment when she wasn't working. She liked quiet and introspection, so isolation wasn't a problem, and she rarely if ever went to fancy restaurants or movies, never bothered with nightclubs, or any kind of instant entertainment the city could offer her. She preferred a home-cooked meal, a movie at home, or reading a good book.

Would losing any of it hurt her? Would losing her independence *matter*, if she had Jim? She'd almost lost him today—

She'd almost lost him. He could have died.

She started shaking again, and sat abruptly.

When Jim followed the other man around to the treatment rooms, she waved them off and stayed in the waiting room. The turbulence in her mind had taken over.

For years she'd allowed the little things about Jim to bother her to the point where she'd stayed well away from him. He was laid-back; she was tense. He laughed his way through life, she was serious. He was messy; she was obsessively neat. He loved meat, coffee and beer; she was a water-and-juice-drinking vegetarian. He was a country boy; she was a city girl. He loved camping; she was terrified of it. He had a big, noisy, loving family; she had only her warring parents.

Yet they'd both worked damn hard to get where they were now, living on a shoestring budget and with part-time work. They'd always competed for top position in class; if they'd hung out at opposite ends of the library, they'd both regularly *been there*. They both loved peace and space, and were united in their love of animals. They both loved the same people….

Neither one could leave those they loved behind.

She'd spent ten years making excuses to keep him at arm's length, because part of her had always known he had the power to take her heart and soul and keep them. Because, while in so many ways they were opposite ends of the spectrum, as he'd said, by some crazy miracle they almost always seemed to reach the same conclusions. They made similar decisions on the big issues.

Were Jim and she so different as she'd always thought?

Suddenly she was impatient to reach her parents' house. If—if he could handle the way they were, and not look at them in horror and wonder if she'd end up the same…

If he could see the woman she might become, and love her anyway…

Take the risk, Danni-girl, her heart whispered. And if Jim's voice in her head was taking over her will, the clamouring of her heart's deepest wish claimed victory over her fierce independence.

Maybe she *was* ready for change.

Danni had something to say.

He could see the nervous indecision in the constant shuffling of her feet, which she only did when she was thinking deeply, the twiddling of her hair, and she kept lifting her fork of Singapore noodles to her mouth, then letting it drop. Peeking at him, then back down at her plate as if it were her refuge.

"Why not just say it?" he asked when she opened and closed her mouth for the fourth time. Whatever it was, it couldn't be as bad as waiting to hear it. "The silence is driving me nuts anyway. Spill, Danni-girl. You'll feel better."

He'd never realised he was so impatient before, but waiting for Danni, when he wanted her, needed her so damn *much*, was making him crazy. Everything was vital. He had to know.

She looked up, with a comical, little-girl bitten lip and wide eyes that made him long to kiss her…though everything she did made him want that these days. "I—I want a date."

Her announcement, somewhere between shy

and aggressive and hauntingly familiar, fell between them like bird droppings splashing into his soup: a strange, half-funny anticlimax. "I assume you mean with me?"

Taking him at face value, she frowned. "Who else would I be asking?"

Refraining from pointing out that she hadn't asked, but demanded, he grinned at her. "Go on."

She lifted a forkful of food again, dropped it and sighed. "It's not that I'm not ready to see my parents. I thought it was that, but it's not. It's just that this week's been so *intense*. It's all been feeling and discovery and change—and passion." That adorable fugitive half smile came and went. "And it's been wonderful, Jim—what's between us, at least. But I need time out." Her gaze on him was earnest. "I need time with *you*. No parents, no travelling, no eating at pit stops or soul searching—just you and me spending the day together."

She didn't say it, but it was there, hovering in the air between them: *being a normal couple*. Jim wanted to smack his forehead for his stupidity. If there was anything he'd learned about Danni in the past week, it was her unending search for normality, and he hadn't even thought of giving her just that.

Suddenly he realised why her tone was familiar: two years ago. The way she'd asked him out then was the same cross between shy admiration and aggression hiding the terror that he'd say *no*.

And he had. He'd made an excuse and bolted, leaving her alone with her rejection and only squabbling parents to fill the void.

Damn it. She was still scared he'd say no? His beautiful Danni reached out to him over and over, expecting nothing in return.

With a teasing smile, he said, "Do we get to hold hands and kiss lots?"

The choked-off giggle was the most enchanting sound he'd ever heard because he'd had to work so hard for it for so many years—and it meant he'd broken the tension coiling inside her. "I think we can negotiate that into the contract."

"Then I'm there. A date for you and me tomorrow. All day. Call your parents, then, and tell them." It would reassure her parents that her life was approaching normal.

Her lashes fluttered down. "Do you mind if I don't tell them why? I want this to be just for you and me."

In case it doesn't work out for us. Danni's place of hiding was popping up again. Fortunately he now knew how to counteract it. "Just you and me," he said softly, lifting her hand to kiss it, tender and lingering.

Her eyes darkened.

Wanting Danni was a pain he'd never known before. He couldn't explain, even to himself, how necessary, how *vital* her presence was to him. Her touch didn't make him just hope they'd soon be sharing a very mutual pleasure. It was wanting to share lives as well as a bed; it was wanting to take on her fears and worries and teach her, *show* her she could let go of them with him. He wanted—no, he *would be* the man she could trust with her heart as well as her body— for life.

So, as much as he ached to make love to her right now—and he knew he had the power to persuade her to take him to her bed—he made himself smile. Danni didn't give her heart, or her body, lightly. She was right: this had been a crazy week, too intense, too catalystic for them both. Danni was ready for change, but she needed time out first.

Maybe he did, too.

If he could make her trust him, she would commit to him—but she needed normality. *They* needed normality together.

They needed their date.

He began to make plans.

CHAPTER ELEVEN

DANNI CLUNG TO THE DOOR HANDLE with both hands, dizzy and terrified. "What on *earth* made you think I'd be interested in something so *crazy*?"

Undeterred, Jim laughed at her, his eyes twinkling. "You flew to Europe, right? You flew around Europe?"

"I sat in the nice safe cabin of a 747, an aisle seat well away from the window! I wasn't in a two-seat Cesspit of Death!"

"The owners of Cessna might object to you calling their two-seaters cesspits. They're really very safe. I've been flying for six years, and never hit a wombat or anything else."

"It's not *funny,* Haskell," she snapped. "This is not my idea of a romantic date!"

And the day had started so well…

Winery visits, buying a champagne picnic for lunch, sharing it on the wide, grassy gardens.

Holding hands and kissing, falling into beautiful, natural passion on the plastic-based blanket;
Jim stopping them just as she'd begun unbutton-
ing his shirt, saying he wasn't that kind of a boy
and she had to give him a ring and tell his family
before he'd give her his body. Making her laugh
without challenge. Relaxing and talking of work,
of friends—carefully avoiding Laila as a topic,
much as they both loved her. Avoiding parental
difficulties.

He'd asked her what her long-term work goals
were, and when she'd admitted she didn't know, it
didn't matter. No lectures, no deep philosophising
on each other's natures or faults—they just had fun.

And then he'd turned into the airport drive…

"The wing's dipping!" she screamed, hanging
onto the handle for dear life.

"It's supposed to. It's cool. I'm just turning
the plane left."

"There's a mountain on the left, right in front
of us!"

He chuckled. "Sorry, Danni, that line's been
taken—and you're not flying the plane. I'm the
aviator here. Let me fly without paranoid inter-
ference, as cute as it is…or you might make
me nervous."

She gasped and closed her mouth, and he chuckled again. "Let go of the door handle—and your fears, baby. I won't let anything happen to you."

Gently, he leaned over her and took a hand. He lifted it to his mouth, kissing her palm and wrist with a sensuality he *knew* she couldn't resist, darn him. "Come on, baby, let go, and just enjoy the experience. Look around you, and see the beauty of being above it all."

"I don't know how you got me in here at all. I should have run in the opposite direction the moment we parked the car," she grumbled, taking an unwilling peek over the dashboard—instrument thingy—whatever.

Okay, it *was* beautiful, the drenched green of the hills and the valley below, the gardens and golf courses and wineries—but they could have explored the beauty from the safety of the ground. Walking…the car…

Safety.

She turned to glare at him. "You planned this, didn't you? They wouldn't normally let another pilot fly. You talked them into it to make a point."

He shrugged, grinning. "Les is an old friend.

He gave me my first twenty hours' flight time. So when I called, he knew I had the skills."

"Are you going to make your point now, or later?" she challenged him.

He turned his face, giving her the warm, intimate, *just-for-Danni* smile that turned her insides to mush. "I don't need to. You were ready to see it for yourself."

I trust him, or I'd never have climbed into the plane.

He knew it; he knew she now knew it. There was nowhere to run from that simple fact, without losing self-respect. Jim had earned her trust. She couldn't take it back now.

Then why am I still so scared? Why can't I let go?

"I don't think you're ready for the whole loop and loss of G-force…right?"

She gasped, both hands returning to the handle.

He laughed and took her right hand back in his. "One day at a time, Danni—and one experience at a time. We have the rest of our lives."

Everything inside her turned to mush at the calm acceptance that he'd be in her life forever—and yet it was too scary. She *wanted* so much….

"We can take on the world one person at a time, one fear at a time," he said softly.

"Good. C-can we get back on the ground now? I think I've enjoyed enough personal growth for one day," she complained, to hide her fears from him. She'd never trusted anyone before, not even Laila. And to believe he could love her forever was a concept her heart and mind couldn't accept. "A massive dose of chocolate sounds really good about now."

"Danni's number-one nerve calmer," he teased. "I could hit the autopilot button and make you forget where we are...."

"Not with that mountain still ahead, you won't." But she knew she was smiling. He had that effect on her.

He's good for me. He makes me feel like—like I'm the same as everyone else.

Just a normal woman in love with her man.

No. It wasn't going to happen. Happily-ever-after was impossible for someone like her.

It was time to go to her parents' house—the place she hadn't called *home* for so long—and face her ghosts, and watch the latter part of *for better or worse* coming early for them.

Spending a lifetime with someone could become a life sentence without real, mutual love, and no one knew that better than she did.

* * *

"Turn right here. The house is the fourth on the right again."

The tension in her voice wasn't anger—it was more like a hopeless kind of acceptance. She knew she was about to be humiliated, and she fully expected him to cut and run.

His beautiful Danni, still with no idea how extraordinary and lovable she was.

Jim turned as directed. He said nothing; there was nothing *to* say. Only going through today, and all the todays with her parents, would convince her of how much he loved and needed her. How she *couldn't* know, with all she'd done for him this week—

It's only been a week. Patience, Haskell!

Strange: it had only been eight days since they'd met again, and yet he'd never once questioned his feelings. From the moment she'd come out to him that first night, the magic she'd always woven around him had become a fatal case; from the first kiss, he'd known his life had changed. He wanted to spend his lifetime loving her.

There were a hundred questions surrounding that: where they'd live; would they work together or separately; how many kids they'd have—

Did she even *want* kids, after her childhood experiences? Though something vital in him would die if he was never a father, the thought of being without Danni was unbearable.

The future questions could wait. Winning her was still the biggest question.

"Pull up here. They'll be out any second." She didn't look at him as she unbuckled her seat belt.

Sure enough, her mother was already running to the car, her father close behind, their faces alight with love and joy—but Danni only looked hunted.

Again, there was nothing to say, nothing she'd accept as truth right now.

She climbed out of the car with a smile so forced, he ached for all three Morrisons. Her mother's joy faded; her beaming face took on a look of imperfectly concealed distress Jim had seen on Danni's face too many times to count. Her father's face remained staunch: a prisoner receiving the expected sentence.

He'd accepted the crimes he'd committed against his daughter, and was doing his time.

All three of them were doing time.

Time to enact the role he knew he did best: the

peacemaker. He closed the car door behind him and walked around to meet her parents, with a big, happy smile he hoped to God concealed his fears a lot better than anyone else was doing.

"Oh, Jim. So nice to meet you properly at last." Margaret Morrison fluttered, half heading to him for a hug, then hesitated, glancing at Danni.

Taking the initiative, he stepped forward and hugged the small, fragile woman first. "It's a real pleasure to meet you, too, Mrs. Morrison." He turned with a smile to Danni's father. "Mr. Morrison. A pleasure, too." He held out his hand; George Morrison shook it.

Then all four of them stood around, in a slightly ridiculous tableau. Jim waited for the invitation into the house, but none came. Finally he took the initiative. "I'd love a glass of water…it's been a long run this morning."

"Yes, of course. We expected you yesterday," Mrs. Morrison said, fluttering around him again. He was reminded of a bird trying to escape a cage.

"Danni says you like a beer."

He grinned at Danni's dad, who was speaking with overdone heartiness. "Yeah, I do—but right now, I'd really love water."

"Hallelujah," he heard Danni mutter to herself,

and he grinned. If it kept her near him, he could handle a few small changes to his diet. She'd been feeding him from her meals all week, and it really wasn't half-bad. He could eat it—now and then.

Mr. Morrison led the way inside, his wife beside him.

The relief on their faces at having gotten past this first hurdle was almost absurd. Had Danni never brought any man home before?

Now he could see where Danni got her intensity from…and why she was so happy to escape it. Their anxiety put a burden on her to reassure them. Could she ever just be her own stroppy, adorable self, free to give or to just relax?

No wonder letting go was so hard for her.

The lunch was just as tight, as concentrated in its unspoken *thinking*. The air was tense with expectation. He had no idea why—what her parents were expecting them to do or say.

Everyone was quiet, punctuated with occasional questions aimed his way, the kind of getting-to-know-you questions that should break the ice, but somehow couldn't manage it.

Danni ate in near-total silence, her head down, picking at the delicious eggplant parmesan, which complimented the barbecue meat her father had made, without any real interest. Every few minutes her gaze flicked to him, gauging his re-actions to her parents' every comment or question.

Waiting for him to make an excuse, cut and run still.

Why do you bother with me?

Now he knew why she'd asked, why she couldn't believe he loved her. She couldn't see beyond her family problems, gave herself no credit for her accomplishments, her unquestion-ing loyalty or her giving, which was deep and selfless, straight from her heart.

Tonight, he'd tell her exactly why he bothered with her, and why he'd be around for the rest of their lives.

Then he realised something. Something unusual, given what he'd seen two years before, and everything Danni had told him.

Apart from the tension, it had been a pleasant lunch. Her parents weren't fighting, or even playing the game of one-upmanship with snide, humiliating comments.

He flicked a glance at Danni, who didn't appear to have noticed. Maybe they were trying to make a good impression on him for Danni's sake; maybe they'd finally gotten the message when she'd stayed away so long.

After lunch, her father cleared his throat, clearly a prelude to something portentous. "Danni, love, your mother and I have something to tell you…."

"I have something to say, too." She pushed her chair back, her face tight. "This is partly my house, too. Grandma left it to us equally. I think it's time you sold up and we all took our shares."

Both her parents stared at her, shock written all over their faces. "You want us to sell the house?" her mother whispered, her hands making that fluttering of distress. "Our *home*?"

"We couldn't afford to buy elsewhere in Sydney—not in this area. We're retired," her father protested.

"Then buy a unit—preferably two—and separate," Danni said bluntly. "Maybe then you can get your own lives and friends, even find someone to love."

"Why would you say this to us?" Her mother was wringing her hands, looking more and more trapped.

"Isn't it obvious?" Weariness lined Danni's every word. "I can't stand this half life as your tennis ball anymore. I'm always bouncing between you both, making excuses for one, apologising for the other. I want you to find your own lives—then I might not feel so warped. I might even finally feel free enough to find a life."

Jim almost couldn't look at her parents now. He felt so sorry for them, but wanted to cheer Danni on. She'd had to take a stand sometime. This wasn't about her, she just wanted to stop the unending war between her parents.

"Well, actually, that's the thing we had to tell you," her father said, his whole bearing tense with nerves. "That last time you shocked us, but you made us both think—enough to talk to each other about what we'd done to you all these years."

"We decided to see a counsellor," Margaret Morrison said. "You were right. We needed help with our issues on forgiving and letting go of the past."

"We had no right to use you that way," George mumbled. "The counsellor has been showing us healthier ways of talking out our feelings the past few months."

Margaret stepped forward to stand beside her

husband. "We, um, started dating a month after our first session."

"To see if there was anything in common besides you," George explained.

"And we found there was, Danielle," her mother said quietly and slipped her hand into her husband's. "We just didn't know…"

"Yes," George agreed, his tone gruff with embarrassment. "We're—used to each other. We're comfortable, and we're learning to be friends."

"We want to give this a really good try, Danielle, to see if we can live in peace in our own house. But I guess now that's up to you." Her mother's pleading gaze fixed on Danni.

Expecting capitulation.

Now it was Danni Jim hardly dared to look at; but the glimpse or two he'd taken had been enough. The utter bewilderment on her face, the disbelief and, yes, distress told a story he was afraid to read.

White with shock, pupils so dilated her eyes seemed black; opening and closing her mouth like an automated machine. The silence stretched out like thin elastic and slowly snapped, and still Danni barely moved and didn't speak. There wasn't a single sign of joy on her face for her parents' fledgling reunion…or was it union?

Jim had no clue what the heck was going on. This was obviously Parents Turn Insane on Their Children without Warning Week.

"I see," she said at last. "Then I guess you'd better do it." She sounded bitter, betrayed.

She got up and walked out of the house without looking back. Her back and shoulders were stiff, but her wandering gait showed the depth of her shock.

George and Margaret Morrison looked at Jim as if he held all the answers to the mystery that was their daughter.

"Congratulations," he said awkwardly. How did he act with his hopeful prospective in-laws at this time? What could he say to them?

"What's the matter with her?" Margaret asked, more bewildered than accusing. "I thought she'd be happy. She *said* she wanted us to stop the fighting…."

"I'm sure she is happy," he said, feeling his way. "But it's all very sudden for Danni. The last time she saw you, I gather it wasn't happy."

"No. It wasn't." George Morrison sounded curt.

Jim swore in silence and stopped talking about

their private business. He had to live with the consequences of whatever he said now.

"I'll go to her," he said quietly. "This has been a real shock to her, given without warning. She needs time to adjust."

"Thank you, Jim," George said, still restrained. "I'm sure it was—a surprise, as you say—but when she came out with wanting to sell the house like that…"

"We'll sell it if that's what she needs. Danielle deserves that from us. Please tell her." Margaret's tone was anxious.

Jim nodded, wondering if Danni's parents had always put their needs onto their daughter without thought of the consequences. They loved Danni dearly, he could see that, by offering to sell the house and meaning it, but years of feeling alone and unloved had left their mark on them both and on Danni. She'd been their referee too long.

It was time, and past time, that Danni became their *daughter*.

"I'm sure she knows, Mrs. Morrison," he replied, trying not to sound as curt as he felt. "It is important that Danni gets her start in life and her career. I'm sure you know that, too," he added, smiling, "and would be willing to come to some arrangement to help her?"

Both the Morrisons looked mildly shocked. "Danielle's always been so independent," Margaret quavered, blinking.

"She never let us lift a finger to help her from the time she was five," George added.

Jim kept his thoughts to himself, saying smoothly, "There's a time for all of us to admit we need a bit of a leg up. We all want security." He left it at that. "Any idea where Danni would go?" No way would she be tamely waiting for him at the car.

"She always went for walks when she wanted—" her mother stopped there, looking as ashamed as she was distressed.

"Peace from our fights," George added heavily. "We haven't done that since the last day she was here. We've begun to change our lives, thanks to Danni."

"I saw that at lunch," Jim said, smiling to reassure them. And then, to make them focus on Danni, he added, "Do you know which way she'd have gone?"

"The waterfront is about half a mile east," George suggested, his eyes troubled. "Head right, down the side street about three doors from here. There's a laneway leading to the river, and a park she always liked, growing up."

Jim nodded. "Don't worry, I'll find her."

CHAPTER TWELVE

DANNI KNEW JIM WOULDN'T BE long in finding her. It didn't matter whether he loved her or had already decided to end it—and she wouldn't blame him if he walked now, given the way she'd just acted—Jim, her gallant knight must find his charger and come to rescue her from her distress.

Sitting by the river on a warm stretch of springy grass, she squinted over the shining waters, deep grey-green dappled with sunlight and reflecting the clear summer sky above. Constant, unchanging and lovely, the river moved on without seeming effort. Nature did what it did: always the same yet always in motion. The seasons changed, water headed for the sea, evaporated and returned as rain. Trees sprouted leaves, they fell and regrew. Fires swept through and destroyed the bush, yet within weeks regeneration began. Healing was the natural order of things.

Why couldn't she do the same? What was *wrong* with her?

This had been the week when all her thoughts, all her most entrenched belief systems were collapsing around her, and she didn't have a single clue what to do with it.

For the first time in her life, she was completely lost.

"Hey."

The breath she didn't know she was holding released itself in relief. He was here. Waiting for Jim had become her obsession the past week. "Hey."

"Can I pull up a patch of grass?"

She shrugged. "Free park."

"There's more that's *free* here than you think," he said quietly as he sat beside her, not touching or attempting to make her smile.

She kept her gaze on the water. Waiting for the words to come.

He knew. He always knew.

"So, do you want to tell me what the house sale demand was about?"

She shrugged again, feeling its repetition—

but right now, originality wasn't high on her list of priorities. "Not the money, if that's what you're thinking."

"I was thinking more along the lines of two things. One, to force their separation so you could get on with your life."

"Bingo," she said dryly.

"And the other," he went on as if she hadn't spoken, "was to force the worst in your parents to come out while I was there. They weren't acting as you expected them to. They hadn't frightened me off. So you said the worst thing you could think of, to show me what they're capable of—and what you're capable of becoming. That you could end up like your mother…right?"

All this holding her breath had to be really bad for her. She sucked in air in a big gasp. Was she really so openly exposed to him? He knew the monsters hiding in her deepest soul, dark terrors she hadn't known were there until he opened the doors to show her.

Her head fell in shame. "Yes," she whispered.

He still hadn't touched her. He spoke with slow precision. "I finally worked it out, walking over here. I thought it was me you didn't trust, that it was me you were testing." He left it there, leaving a hole in the silence so large she wanted to run through it and disappear. "You didn't know what to do when your parents didn't act true to form."

She didn't answer; it wasn't really a question.

"It had to have been a shock, them announcing their reconciliation like that."

She sighed. "They never *conciled* in the first place *to* reconcile…at least, never in my memory."

"Okay," was all he said, his tone cautious. Willing to humour her. "So it looks like they might find love late in life—or at least friendship. That's wonderful…isn't it?"

"I don't know," she murmured, lost, forlorn. "Is it?"

"After all these years, they could end up happy. They certainly look happier than the people I saw in Bathurst."

Happy? What was that? Not something she'd had in her vocabulary when it came to her own life, let alone her parents'. "So I'll go get the champagne and toast the bride and groom, throw a celebration party for their marriage, about thirty years too late."

"Thirty years too late for whom, Danni?" he asked softly, with meaning.

She closed her eyes. "For the little girl who doesn't know how to believe it can last. For the girl who believes love is pain and humiliation in public, and all her friends thinking it was so funny when they'd seen my parents fighting. Or scary, and they never came to play again." She sighed. "It's too late for the warped child inside me, Jim."

"It isn't me you don't trust, is it?" he repeated, turning her face so she had to look at him. "It's you."

"Yes," she burst out in a repressed whisper, because unlocking her soul aloud was too damn scary. "How can I not end up like them, Jim? How can I expect anyone to love me for long, when I don't even know if I love my own parents half the time?"

Leaving his hand under her chin, he whispered back, just as fiercely, "You apply your psychology to everyone except yourself. Hate the behaviour, not the people. Get angry with what they do, not with them. And so what if you're like them?"

She felt the first tear spill over her cheek and run down into his hand with a sense of fatality. Her self-control seemed to have passed into his keeping with her secrets. "If their own daughter runs away from them all the time…"

"I'm going to leave, is that it? You don't trust yourself to be Miss Sweetness and Light all the time, so you can't believe that I'll stay."

The fierceness in his eyes and voice took her aback. "How can I, Jim? You tell me how I can believe you'll want to stay with me, if I turn into my mother?"

To her shock, his mouth twitched. "I have bad news for you, Danni—you already *are* your mother."

She gasped. "How *dare* you say that? I've tried so hard—all my life—"

"Too bad. Genetics is a game of tag, you're it. You're your mother. So what?"

"So—so…" She floundered into silence.

"So I can't love you for long, because your dad never loved your mother?" He mirrored her thoughts with frightening accuracy. When she nodded in weary defeat, he went on, "But there are three major differences in our scenario. I like your mother, so I don't see that as a problem. I'm already in love with you, just as you are—and *I'm not your father*. I don't shut you out every time you reach out to me, and I'll never give you cause for jealousy. You'll never get a chance to turn bitter on me, Danni, or doubt how much I love you."

She couldn't get past his assertion that she was her mother. She wanted to hit him, to scream and yell and deny what he'd said, but it was her greatest fear and deepest-hidden belief held up as a mirror to her soul, and she couldn't lie. Not anymore. Denial did nothing to change the truth. "No. I know you're going to get tired of me sooner or later, and—"

"Have you spent your whole life blaming your mother for the failure of their marriage?" he asked gently.

"What?" She blinked. "I—I don't understand."

"For how many years have you thought to yourself, 'If Mum was nicer to Dad, if she was a different person, we would all have been happy,' or thoughts similar?"

Now she was gaping. "I—always," she whispered, shocked to the core. *He knew...*

"So even though your dad used your mum to forget another woman, he doesn't get any blame? Even though he never tried to make her happy, and wasn't nice to her, even in front of you?" He still spoke in tender understanding. "Have you always sided with your dad? Have you never wondered if your mum's bitterness came from being lonely—that she was never good enough for either of you?"

The wisdom sank into her soul, touching the very core of her: the cold numbness of blame the child Danni had laid during the first fight she could remember hearing. *It was true*. She'd spent most of her life siding with her father, giving her mother the unconscious blame, time and time again. If she hadn't gotten pregnant... If she hadn't told him about it...

But it takes two to make a baby—just as it takes two to destroy a marriage. She'd blamed her mother because it was the easiest solution. She'd sided with Dad to prove to herself she was *not* her mother's daughter. *She* would never trap a man into marriage and force him to stay there.

But Dad had been faced with the same dilemma, had made the same choices, made all the same mistakes—and now, he was taking responsibility for it.

As was Mum. The change in them both had been shining like a beacon all day—no, really, with every phone call they'd made in the past few weeks. Yet, focussed on everything she'd always hated about them both, she'd been blind to every sign of change.

Dad wants to stay with Mum. He—he must care....

Did that mean her mother wasn't as unlovable as she'd always thought?

That she, Danni, wasn't as unlovable as she'd always feared?

That her father had just as much fault in the problems between them was a revelation to her, and it tore the blinders from her soul.

Was it too late for love? Was it too late for conciliation, and reconciliation for her parents? They didn't think so....

They were changing...then so could she. Wasn't that what Jim was telling her? Could she lay the foundation for a better relationship with them both—one that would be far healthier than the polite evasions and endurance of the past twenty years? Was it too late for her to forgive them from the heart for all those years of damage?

To believe love can happen...?

If she kept hanging onto her old beliefs, holding onto her fears, sooner or later she'd lose Jim. And losing Jim would hold a lifetime of regret. No amount of safety could ever fill the emptiness of never again seeing his smile, hearing his unorthodox wisdom, feeling the warmth of his arms and body, or the soaring joy of his kiss.

It couldn't be too late. She wouldn't let it be! With Jim standing beside her, she could do it all. She could be the woman she'd always ached to become—no longer looking at life from a cold window, but from inside it, warm and happy—contented and loved.

So do it. Take the leap of faith....

Her parents had made the change, and they *did* seem happier than she'd ever seen them. Couldn't she do the same? Could she trust Jim to love her through the bad times sure to come to her?

I'm not your father. I won't shut you out.

"Well?" came the tender, remorseless voice of her conscience, the man who loved her enough to show her the truth. "Can you stop funding their war, go back in there and wish them happiness from your heart?"

She gulped, and gulped again. Ashamed, so shamed and wilfully blind and stupid all these years! She'd called Jim an enabler, but she'd been the one to keep the family war alive by taking sides. Dad wasn't a hero, and Mum wasn't a villain. They were just people who wanted a second chance—just as she wanted hers. With Jim.

It was time to leave the darkness—

No, it wasn't there to leave. Jim had poured warmth and light into her places of hiding, taking away the fear. She was already in the light.

She was already in the light. Because of Jim. Her wonderful, beautiful Jim….

"C-can we buy some champagne?" she whispered.

The sternness in his eyes melted. "I knew you could do it. I'm so proud of you."

She lowered her face. "I don't know what they want from me. I don't know what to say or do."

"Just let them into your life, Danni. All they want is to be loved. You can do it." He tipped her face up and kissed her, sweet and deep. "You're the one that made them see the need for change. You knew what to do—and you did it before I came back into your life. You made the leap all by yourself, and you did it for their sakes, not just your own."

She buried her face in his neck, feeling a twenty-year burden slide from her shoulders.

Her parents no longer wanted the war, they just wanted her to be happy for them.

She was free, at last. Free to find happiness.

He'd given her the gift of a lifetime, with those simple words. With the love and faith drenched in everything he said to her, in every look and touch.

I'm already in the light. She was happy—and she wanted to stay that way forever.

Drawing in a shaking breath, she tried to think of the right words to say. *You're the most beautiful thing to have happened to me. Thank you, thank you for everything you are....*

"Will you marry me?" she whispered instead, and heard him gasp. But all she felt was a brilliant, soaring gladness. The freedom to fly she'd yearned to know all her life had always been inside her. She'd just needed a catalyst; someone to show her where her wings had been hiding.

She'd needed Jim, a man who wasn't afraid to give from the heart, even when his own life was falling apart. A man who knew he didn't have to break down her walls and barriers; he just turned the key in the lock and walked right in where he belonged, bringing sunshine and laughter to counterbalance her darkness—and yes, to give her a belief in herself for the first time.

Hope. Jim was her hope, her light and joy—her future. Because he believed in her. Because he *loved* her…and because she finally believed a man, *her man*, was here for life.

"I love you so much," she said softly, wrapping her arms around his waist. "I think I've loved you since first year—or maybe second year, that's when I wanted you to notice me, and resented—anyway, will you marry me? Please? I know I won't be easy to live with, but I will always try to make sure you never regret—"

"After years of the silent treatment, now I can't get the woman to shut up long enough to accept her proposal," he teased, lifting her face again. His face was—incandescent. Alight with the same joy blazing in her soul. "I thought I'd need to wait two or three years to get you to the point where you'd accept I was here for life."

"You forget, I've been in this thing ten years," she laughed, giddy with the joy she'd never expected to know. "It might be new for you, but I've been lusting after you for a very long time, Haskell."

"Ditto, Danni-girl." His gaze drank in her face, with that big-as-the-desert grin she adored. "I was just blind to what it really was for years. It would have been different if I'd known it was returned. If you'd told me before last week…say, a few years ago…"

"Well, it doesn't help when you try and the man bolts at a hundred miles an hour," she teased. Then she nuzzled his cheek and kissed him once, twice. "I'm ready to believe in us, to accept this is forever. If I hadn't been ready, nothing would have made me go with you to meet your family—or to have you meet mine."

"I knew that all along." He grinned again. "Do you think I'd have turned caveman on you if I thought you wouldn't like it? You were just a bit slow to see it, that's all."

She laughed and shoved him until he fell to the ground. She landed on him, kissing him over and over, whispering words of love.

"And for the record, I'm pretty sure I started falling for you the day I rescued you from the sleaze at graduation," he mumbled between kisses. "I only began to know it when my date the other night pointed out that it was *you* I couldn't stop looking at. When I looked again, it felt as if I'd always been looking at you, always wanting you."

The joy in her heart overflowed, but she couldn't resist teasing him. "Jim the heroic knight strikes again. It took rescuing me to know you loved me. I wonder if we'd be here now if it weren't for the sleaze. Maybe I should go and thank him."

"You stay away from that weasel," he growled, and she laughed.

He rolled over until he was lying beside her. He leaned on one elbow, playing with her hair with his free hand. "I know life won't always be easy with you, Danni, but it's not as if sharing my life and family will be a picnic. And though I know it'll take at least another year to get you to the altar, that's okay, too. I like challenges," he teased, "and I'd be bored to tears with a placid life. I want *you*, smart mouth, challenges and all." He turned serious and tender. "I love you, Danni, and I'm so proud of you."

She lay back on the grass, smiling up at him, trying to hold back the tears. "I think I'm proud of me, too. I've come a long way."

He leaned over and kissed her, deep, slow and sensuous, until she moaned and pulled him down onto her, aching for him. "Have you come far enough to make another leap of faith? Will you come and live the outback life with me?"

"Huh?" Dazed with desire, she couldn't think.

She wanted him so much…she tugged him back down to her. "Kiss me again."

Chuckling softly, he murmured, "Greedy woman you are."

They were both mussed and breathless with passion when they finally stopped. "We're in a public park," he whispered when she moaned her protest. "We're almost at indecent exposure here."

"Unfair," she grumbled, moving her hands under his shirt. "I wait twenty-nine years for this to come along—and ten years for *you* to notice me—and you keep putting me off."

He held her hands as she tried to kiss him again. "This is serious, Danni. I have to know if you'll share my life. I'm committed to my practice in Cooinda for at least the next five years."

She frowned and tilted her head, then began shaking her head in adoration. "You think I'm dumb or something, Haskell? My gallant knight never surrenders his post. I knew that when I proposed—and I'm tired of city life and temp vetting. Can you use a partner?"

"Could I use—" He grabbed her and kissed her. "My beautiful Danni-girl, you'd be the partner from heaven. I knew I'd keep on finding good reasons why I love you. I was dreading heading back tomorrow to the locum who is no doubt having a nervous breakdown from one week of my workload. I'm the only vet for about two hundred kilometres each way, and the lack of sleep is slowly driving me bonkers. Sharing the load means the occasional day off...."

"No, control freak of mine," she teased, loving the sound of *mine* on her lips when it came to Jim. "It means I work beside you to get the jobs done faster, so we can spend more time together." She moved sensuously against him to make her point.

Their kiss soon turned hot, broken by the afternoon screeching of a cockatoo—and just as well, as Jim pointed out unsteadily, since they were still in public.

"Speaking of together," he said, abandoning the practicalities of their practice, which they could hammer out later, "let's go pick out an engagement ring before the stores shut. Then we can go back and give your parents the good news."

She groaned. "Do we have to tell them now? They'll start nagging about church weddings and grandchildren within minutes."

"Yeah, yeah, and you'll want to do the exact opposite, just to prove you can. Too bad, Morrison. You proposed—but I get to give you the ring—so you're stuck with me now." He laughed and kissed her. "Compromise is part of family life. My parents will have a Goodoona wedding and at least four grandkids planned by the time we get back home. We can smile and ignore them all, you know. Or we tell them to shut up or we'll elope—said in all love and respect, of course." He grinned at her. "I can show you a hundred ways of making the family happy while doing exactly what we want to do."

Clink. More chains fell from her soul. Who would have believed that with love came, not more burdens, but such glorious freedom? "I adore you," she whispered, choking on joy and laughter.

His eyes darkened. "Then let's get that engagement ring. I want to bind you to me as fast and tight as possible. I'll never let you run from me again. If you want to go anywhere from now on, I go with you."

She touched his face. "You still don't know, do you? All you ever had to do these past ten years was put your hand out to me, and I'd have gone anywhere with you."

With a smile, he got to his feet and put out his hand. "Let's go, then."

Smiling back with all the love she felt inside, she put her hand in his.

EPILOGUE

Cabarita Park, Sydney, two years later

"MOVE IN A LITTLE CLOSER. That's it. Good!" The photographer beamed. "Now smile, everyone. I love these extended family weddings."

The shutter whirred again, taking the bride and groom, and all six parents, before Annie and Mick faded quietly back into the larger family group.

Danni leaned on him. "I am *so* tired of these photos."

Claire twitched Danni's veil. "You okay?"

Jim smiled at his adopted mother. Two years had made the situation more comfortable than he'd have believed at the start of this crazy roller coaster; so much so that while Annie and Mick were mostly hovering in the background, they were *here*. As were Jackie and Sean, his birth brother and sister, standing around chatting to his other brothers and sisters as the cousins they were. "She's just tired. It's been a long day."

Claire snorted. "Okay, keep your secret a bit longer. I can keep my mouth shut, but Margie and George are desperate to be grandparents, so it won't last long." She kissed them both, winked and wandered over to his dad to fix his tie, which he'd tugged askew again.

"Do you think they all know?" Danni whispered, looking around at all their parents.

He grinned and kissed her. "At the rate you've been eating *my* ice cream, I'd say so."

"*Our* ice cream." She rubbed a hand over her belly, which hadn't yet sprung from its customary flatness, but at over three months, it had to happen soon. "Well, at least they don't know our other secret. And they never will," she added firmly.

"Laila does, I think." He turned and winked at their mutual best friend, who had her hands full stopping Ally and little Jessica from running down into the river. She'd been wrong about that boy, too, but Jake had their four-week-old son Adam cradled in his arms. "She's asked a lot of questions about our Fiji trip last year."

"She knows everything, that woman. She knew I loved you before I did, too. Centuries ago they'd have burned her—but at least she'll keep it to herself, or only tell Jake." Danni leaned more into him, less from tiredness than love. "Happy anniversary," she whispered.

This day was actually the first anniversary of their beach wedding in Fiji. Neither of them had wanted this kind of ceremony, or to be surrounded by people while they made very private vows. So they'd skipped to Fiji and married on a beach on the Korolevu Coast, barefoot and in simple island clothing. They'd had the honeymoon of a lifetime on a private island resort, snorkelling and scuba diving, eating, wandering the beach and making love.

That had been *their* dream wedding—and so long as they didn't tell anyone, nobody would be hurt by their private choices. Their wedding day remained their delicious secret.

Today and tomorrow were the family celebrations, their gift to those they loved, and the kind of ceremony the families wanted. Today was Sydney, the church ceremony and the shots at Danni's beloved waterfront park to please her parents. Tomorrow they all headed to Goodoona, and the simple backyard garden wedding favoured by his family. And if the Fiji "honeymoon" was really an anniversary trip, again, what everyone didn't know…

It was as he'd taught Danni: there were loads of ways to compromise while getting what you wanted.

He smiled down at the wife who adored both him and their frenetic outback life, who was ecstatic to be carrying their first child—she'd lost her fears of parenthood with him by her side. What one of them lacked, the other made up for. That would give balance and strength to any and all kids they had.

Danni had come such a long way…and so had he.

They loved his family with all its mess. They both shared a new closeness with her parents, who were holding hands in quiet affection. They were friendly with Annie and Mick—and yes, they'd given them a deposit for the little country house his birth parents had wanted. Sean and Jackie had helped out, as had his parents, so that the bank had given Annie and Mick a small loan for the rest.

Danni had roped them all into it.

But then, that was his Danni. Her heart, once cracked open, had begun opening wider for each new person that came into their lives, for each animal that needed their care. She'd finally learned to trust. And once she knew how, she gave it her all, in her usual unstinting manner. Danni was most truly his partner, in every way. Opposite ends of the spectrum had met in the middle, creating a rainbow he could never have envisioned in his personal sky a few years ago.

He had everything he could want in life, and then some.

"Happy anniversary–wedding day, Danni-girl." He dipped her over his arm, and as her simple veil floated across her face, he kissed her through it, laughing.

And the beaming photographer captured the moment for posterity.

MILLS & BOON PUBLISH EIGHT LARGE PRINT TITLES A MONTH. THESE ARE THE EIGHT TITLES FOR NOVEMBER 2007.

BOUGHT: THE GREEK'S BRIDE
Lucy Monroe

THE SPANIARD'S BLACKMAILED BRIDE
Trish Morey

CLAIMING HIS PREGNANT WIFE
Kim Lawrence

CONTRACTED:
A WIFE FOR THE BEDROOM
Carol Marinelli

THE FORBIDDEN BROTHER
Barbara McMahon

THE LAZARIDIS MARRIAGE
Rebecca Winters

BRIDE OF THE EMERALD ISLE
Trish Wylie

HER OUTBACK KNIGHT
Melissa James

 MILLS & BOON®
Pure reading pleasure

1007 Rom LP

MILLS & BOON PUBLISH EIGHT LARGE PRINT TITLES A MONTH. THESE ARE THE EIGHT TITLES FOR DECEMBER 2007.

———————— ❧ ————————

TAKEN: THE SPANIARD'S VIRGIN
Lucy Monroe

THE PETRAKOS BRIDE
Lynne Graham

THE BRAZILIAN BOSS'S INNOCENT MISTRESS
Sarah Morgan

FOR THE SHEIKH'S PLEASURE
Annie West

THE ITALIAN'S WIFE BY SUNSET
Lucy Gordon

REUNITED: MARRIAGE IN A MILLION
Liz Fielding

HIS MIRACLE BRIDE
Marion Lennox

BREAK UP TO MAKE UP
Fiona Harper

 MILLS & BOON®
Pure reading pleasure

1107 Rom L